GARkY MICHAEL

All The Cuts And Scars We Hide

Copyright © 2021 by Garry Michael

All rights reserved. No part of this publication may be reproduced, stored or transmitted in any form or by any means, electronic, mechanical, photocopying, recording, scanning, or otherwise without written permission from the publisher. It is illegal to copy this book, post it to a website, or distribute it by any other means without permission.

This novel is entirely a work of fiction. The names, characters and incidents portrayed in it are the work of the author's imagination. Any resemblance to actual persons, living or dead, events or localities is entirely coincidental.

First edition

Cover art by Roopali's Creation
Editing by E.B. Slayer
Editing by Carlie Slattery

This book was professionally typeset on Reedsy.
Find out more at reedsy.com

To the men and women in uniform, past, present, and future, thank you for your service and sacrifice.

Acknowledgement

I take great pleasure extending gratitude where it is due. Mr. Z, thank you for your love and support. This journey was made perfect with you by my side.

To my family and friends. THANK YOU!

To my team, Carlie Slattery, E.B Slayer and Roopali. Thank you for sharing your talent with me. Wyatt and Kai's story came full circle because of your guidance.

To my good friend Ebony, thank you for turning me into a "Description Ho". I appreciate you. To Jeris Jean, you have been the book of knowledge whenever I have a writing/advertising question. I can't wait to see where our partnership will take us. Thank you!

To Ms. Mock AKA Christy and Michaela Cole, you have been so generous with your time and talent. Our community is so lucky to have both of you.

Thank you! To Lyndsay. Tina, Dawn and Britanny, my OG gals, you've been with me from the VERY beginning. Thank you for welcoming me with open arms and your continued support.

To Elle Bor, thank you for allowing me to use your amazing poem. Your words are stunning.

To CM Danks, Tempest Phan, Lizzie Stanley, Janice Jarrell, Charm White, Zee Shine Storm, Swati MH, Skylar Platt, N Dune, Eve Riley, Sue Watts, PK Morrison and every independent author out there, the kindness and support you've shown this newbie is more than I could have ever asked for. Sorry in advance if I failed to mention your name. Please know that I appreciate you!

To all the bloggers, influencers and book fanatics who helped me spread the word about All The Cuts and Scars We Hide, Thank you. This is for you.

To Sam and Dar, Thank you for your unyielding love and support.

To Elly and Reenie, thank your for always cheering for me from a far. I appreciate you!

To my ARC readers, thank you for taking the time to read and review this work of mine. I'll be forever grateful.

Last but not the least, the readers. Thank you for your continued support, not just for me, but for every independent author out there. This is for you!

Trigger Warning!

A very detailed war scene, including an IED explosion, and characterization of PTSD are depicted in this novel. If you are suffering from any mental illness that could be triggered by these events, please proceed with caution.

ALL THE CUTS AND SCARS WE HIDE

From the Ashes Series Book One
by
Garry Michael

Healing

I am constantly in a race with time
a wager between who can mend me first
its hand or mine
Yet healing is just as uncanny
as the genesis of our pain
Always an enigma
in purpose and origin
Cannot be forced
Hard to beacon
But when it arrives,
it lacks the promise of permanence

And I wish I knew that
before I picked at my scabs
then wondered why my wounds
still bleed

By Elle Bor

One: Wyatt

The Ambush And Its Aftermath

"Ambush!" *Staff Sergeant Bennett yelled while bullets tore through the air. Our feet scrambled as we ran for cover, combat boots pounding, hearts thumping, the incessant clang of metal on metal as shots pierced through cars lining the deserted streets. The crumbling concrete and barrage of grenades dropped around our perimeter created a dust storm that was impossible to see through.*

"Lance Corporal!" Martinez yelled.

I looked all around to find Private First-Class James "Jim" Martinez.

A partial dispersion of smoke appeared twenty feet north of where I was standing, and I saw him sitting behind an abandoned vehicle with broken glass windows and all the paint removed from old explosions. He held his right leg, covered with blood seeping through his pants, his face daubed with agony and fear. He was cradling his gun close to his chest while he signed the cross repeatedly.

"Martinez, stay down!" I yelled to get his attention and motioned my hand low to advise him to keep out of sight. I hadn't yet made the first step in his direction, when someone yanked my pack, pulling

me backward before another explosive hit near our location, debris exploding around us, missing us entirely.

I blew out a breath when I realized how close we were from being incinerated by another bomb. "Fuck!" I turned around to find our Staff Sergeant beneath me. "Thank you," I murmured in between coughs caused by the smoke and ash floating around in the air. I knew I couldn't get to Martinez then because it was too dangerous.

He tapped my shoulder and I peeled myself off him. With his justifiably shaky hands, he turned on his radio and placed another call for backup. "We need to find cover, keep going south," he screamed, ordering the crew who followed us. But with all the gunfire noises coming from every direction, accompanied by loud native music to confuse us, they couldn't hear him, much less understand his commands.

One by one, my fellow soldiers were taken down by snipers nestled on top of the dozens of abandoned buildings around Kabul. They undoubtedly had been expecting us. With the window of opportunity to counterstrike narrowed down, we started firing, aiming for nothing and no one in particular while we pulled and carried every live body we could find.

Once we found safe harbor in one of the dilapidated buildings, we assessed our situation. Our commander looked around counting how many of our guys managed to get there. "Fuck! Fuck! Fuck!" he cursed as he loosened his bulletproof vest and sat back against the wall, leaning his head down, looking defeated.

I peeked outside and judging by the sheer amount of gunshots fired, we were outnumbered. The shooting momentarily stopped, and cries of anguish echoed through the canyon of the destroyed buildings as we perused our surroundings for our enemies within our confinement.

"Three o'clock!" someone yelled.

ONE: WYATT

Instinctively, I aimed toward that direction. With my vantage point behind a wall, hidden from our attackers, I took them one at a time. But for every Taliban soldier I'd taken down, a couple more appeared to take their place.

An enemy fighter shouted in Pashto and pointed toward me.

"Shit!" My cover was blown. I ducked behind the wall as shots flew my way. Vibrations rumbled through it and I felt the concrete starting to give out. "Goddamn it!" I said, an understanding of my current predicament becoming clear.

The Taliban started to make their move, surrounding our location, when a new brigade of soldiers, that Staff Sergeant Bennett called for backup assistance, cornered the street a couple of blocks from where we were stranded. More shots were fired followed by the whoop of a grenade being launched.

The explosion knocked me to my hands and knees.

My ears were ringing when I scrambled to take cover. I peeked around the remnants of the wall and was relieved to see more of our troops and a battalion of allies had joined the chaos. Back up had arrived.

Marine Corps helicopters hovered above us firing rounds of shots, while fighter jets dropped more bombs, suffocating the Taliban from the ground and the air.

When the enemy finally retreated, we searched around the carnage for live bodies. Gunfire and shouting were replaced by anguished calls echoing through the deserted town adorned with bullet holes.

"Wyatt."

I combed the street covered with bullet shells, broken glass, and blood for the source of Martinez's voice. Relieved that my friend was still alive, I hurried toward him, stepping over our fallen comrades to help. He was in bad shape with multiple gunshot wounds to his right leg and torso. "*Can you stand up?*" *I asked.*

He just nodded, a grimace on his face.

I propped him up and draped his right arm around me for leverage. "Hang in there, buddy," I said to him as we navigated our way to the military vehicle that would take us to our camp.

"*IED!*" *someone yelled from a distance and my world exploded before I could take my next step.*

An orange ball of fire propelled me twenty feet away. Pain pierced through my skin and screamed through my eardrums. I laid there in shock, eyes wide open. The air above me was thick with smoke and debris falling from the sky like snow on a winter's day. My breathing became more labored and I fought not to lose consciousness. I gave my body commands, starting with my right arm, then my left. Relieved that both my arms were intact, I did the same with my legs. I said a small prayer when both of them reacted.

I propped my head up to find where Martinez had landed and then I saw his body. What was left of it anyway. "Jim!" I screamed. I couldn't think. I could barely breathe. Heavy footsteps closed in on me and I heard them say my name.

"*We got you Lance Corporal, you're safe now," someone said.*

I let the darkness take me.

* * *

I woke up gasping for air. My mouth was dry and my whole body was still trembling from the nightmare that had plagued me the past four years. I reached for my neck to feel the chain with Jim's tag over mine.

I attempted to steady my breathing and laid my shaking

ONE: WYATT

hands on the bed, palms down. The light blue sheet was wrinkled and damp. The cold breeze coming from the slightly opened window did nothing to cool my body as more sweat seeped out of me.

"It's just a dream. It's just a dream. It's just a dream." I kept repeating, trying to get me out of the dark cloud that had taken over me. My heart knew that it was a dream, but my mind seemed to have a harder time believing what was reality.

Without any desire to go back to sleep, I forced myself out of bed, headed to the living room, and braced myself for the aftermath. And based on my previous episodes, I knew the shockwave of imminent gloom would soon claim me for the next few hours. Hours that seemed like days, weeks, even eternity.

I summoned all of what was left of my energy to practice the 'Counting Method'. It was the very first technique I'd learned during the early sessions I had with my therapist, Dr. Tina A. McAndrew. Never had counting from zero to a hundred felt so taxing than at that very moment. I accompanied every integer with deep breaths building a sense of rhythm. But after a few failed attempts, I gave up. More tears slipped down my cheeks to my lips. Tasting each defeat, I realized that once again, PTSD won the fight.

The stranglehold this affliction had on me grew tighter like a vice grip as the night sky gave way to the morning sun. I shuddered to think how many more of these events were headed my way. Especially this time of the year.

With just enough will and motivation left in me, I unlocked my phone to send my friend and business partner, Elizabeth, a text. I quickly went through my mental Rolodex of excuses, searching for a reason that required the minimal explanation.

I had an emergency and will not make it to work. Please have Avery sail the charter for me. I'll talk to you later.

After pressing send, I turned off my phone and stared at the loneliness of the room that matched my heart.

It was now Monday and it had been three days since my last episode and I was still reeling from the aftermath. I had sequestered myself to the four corners of my room and only got out of bed to get something to drink and even that was few and far between.

Forcing myself up, I went to the bathroom to attempt to rid myself of this overwhelming malaise. I flicked on the switch and the bright light assaulted my sight. I closed my eyes to cut the sharp pain that was blinding me, a reminder of how long it had been since I'd seen any light. I opened my eyes slowly, allowing them to adjust to the piercing brightness. When I did, I stood in front of the mirror and studied the man standing right in front of me. His face was haunted and pale with bloodshot eyes staring back at me. I reached to touch my face and blinked my eyes and the man in the mirror mimicked each gesture.

His grey eyes were dulled by the dark circles around them and his blank stare made him look dead inside. I leaned over to the cool white porcelain sink while grabbing its edge and shut my eyes for a few seconds, seconds that turned into minutes while I took long heavy breaths. I tried to think of anything other than the hollowness, but each memory was splintered by the nightmares, replacing the few happy memories I had with the ones I buried deep inside the darkest corner of my mind.

ONE: WYATT

I opened my eyes and lifted my head to face the man staring in front of me, my reflection somewhat looked familiar, a fraction of the man I once knew.

Small victory.

I powered through shaving under the scalding hot shower, pleased to feel anything other than the dull ache that had taken residence in my mind, body, and soul these past few days. I stayed under the massaging spray until the water was freezing cold.

I finished my fourth cup of coffee since I woke up an hour ago, but the coffee I'd hoped to get me going might as well have been water since all it managed to accomplish was to make me pee. My lack of enthusiasm this morning was more crippling than usual and I had to drag myself to my truck. And that was something coming from me. Luckily, I was my own boss and enthusiasm was low on my priority list.

The sound of the metal folding when the garage door opened made my stomach drop. I turned the volume of the car stereo louder to drown out the noise, "You're okay, you're okay, you're okay." Thankful that my quick band-aid worked, I turned the car ignition with my trembling hand, took deep breaths, and drove.

I pulled over on a private road three miles north of town in front of a nondescript beige building. There were a total of eight cars idling in the parking lot. And once the clock struck eight o'clock, people started climbing out of their cars to head inside. I debated whether or not to follow them or do what I'd done so often, drive away.

This would have been my forty-third support group session if I'd manned up and followed through with a program designed to help me cope. But out of the forty-three sessions that passed, I only managed to attend eight of them. And those days that I was able to make it, I'd always expected them to kick me out of the program because of my inability to commit. Even when participation was encouraged, I just sat there and listened. But Jason, the support group leader, just looked at me with understanding and told me he'd see me next time. It's not that I didn't try, because I did. And before I talked myself out of driving away, yet again, I got out of the car and entered the building, hoping that this session would be different from the last.

Two: Kai

I'm not in Hawai'i Anymore

Sailboats in different colors and sizes passed by, floating like red and white butterflies in the bay. Waves crashed over the rocky beach of the San Juan Islands, spraying mists of salty water on my face. In the seven days since I'd arrived from Oahu, I had to constantly stop myself from booking the next flight home.

I can't go back.

I could still hear my cousin Mikaela's voice in my head. *You can't run away from this Kai. You can put distance between us, but you can't run away from this, not even if you move to Mars tomorrow.*

I shook my head and focused on the present, a task that was easier said than done, especially when the past was the very reason for the present.

Everything around this island was different. The color of the cold water was a darker shade of blue compared to the warm turquoise ocean I learned how to swim in when I was younger. Towering black rocks dominated the dark brown beach, a far cry from the white powder we used to build sandcastles with and relax on after hours of surfing. Even the waves were tamer than the ones I used to ride. The morning breeze was cooler than the tropical ones I used to wake up to. But what it offered that Hawai'i couldn't, was the fresh start I needed.

I blinked away the tears that were starting to form and reminded myself of why I was standing on a beach twenty-five hundred miles away from home.

Fresh start.

I took my shoes and socks off and rolled my pants past my ankles, walked closer to the waves, and dipped my feet to feel the water. The ice-cold temperature of it caused me to shiver and I immediately retreated them from the freezing shore. *I'm definitely not in Hawai'i anymore* and that thought sobered me more than the bone-chilling water temperature. *I'm on my own now.*

I ran toward the driftwood log where I'd put my shoes and socks and hurried to put them back on. I continued my walk toward the wooden boardwalk which was half the size of a football field. I passed by a couple heading in the opposite direction and waved at them because I needed some form of human acknowledgment. The one thing that was the same between Hawai'i and this island was the people. They all seemed to be friendly and kind even to newcomers like me.

I decided to head out to the coffee shop called *The Sound Café* to try some of the local treats. My landlord, Sam, had recommended it when I asked her about a great place for coffee when I picked up my keys in her office in one of the buildings along Main Street.

* * *

TWO: KAI

"You should check out The Sound Café two blocks south of the boardwalk. They're one of the best on the island," she announced proudly. To my surprise, she leaned closer and held my arm, the jasmine scent of her perfume reminding me of Ma's. "Starbucks moved in a couple of years ago and they couldn't even compete. They tried, but we Islanders support each other, you know," she whispered as if giving me the island's best-kept secret. The wrinkles on the sides of her eyes deepened when she gave me the sweetest smile.

"That's good to know. Thanks for the tip."

"Of course, Kai, you're one of us now. Where'd you park?" She craned her neck and her beautiful locks flowed around her shoulders. It was hard to tell how old she was. She could be in her forties or fifties, but her smile and the way she was put together with a loose short sleeve emerald silk blouse tucked into a pair of skinny dark denim jeans finished with the dark green heels made her look younger. Whatever her age, she looked fabulous.

"Um, I don't drive," I swallowed the lump that was forming in my throat and ignored how my stomach turned to knots at the mention of driving. "Airport shuttle dropped me off."

"Oh, you're not moving in until later then?" she asked, confusion drawn on her face.

"No, I'm moving in today. This is all I have," I explained, pointing at the two oversized, packed to the brim, luggage and the duffle bag sitting on top of one of them.

My cellphone in my back pocket vibrated and a notification popped up on my watch. "And my bed and couch are on its way," I said and showed her the message on my Apple Watch.

She smiled once again while shaking her head. "You millennials are something else. I've always wanted one of those, but my kids can't seem to find the time to teach me." Hurt flashed across her

11

face briefly before she schooled her expression.

"You know what, it's very user-friendly. It's a bit intimidating at first, but it's very easy to learn," I took my watch off my wrist and turned it on, and showed her.

She stood closer to my side, her eyes bouncing from me to the watch as I explained.

"You can tap this button to show your apps, then to go back, you just hit this."

"Just like an iPhone," her eyes wide as she grinned.

"Exactly like it. You can sync your iPhone with it. If you like, I can help you set it up if you still want one of these."

"Oh, Kai. I don't want to impose."

"Not at all, think of it as a bribe. I'm going to need a lot of help learning about this town."

"You're sweet. I hope you make Friday Harbor your new home. The ladies will love you. Athletically built, dark, and handsome."

"Do you think guys will like me too?" I winked. I'd always been comfortable with my sexuality, but I didn't know how a small town like Friday Harbor in the San Juan Islands treated gays. This beautiful coastal town was only hours from Seattle, one of the most progressive cities in the US, but it was hard to know. I held my breath as I awaited her response.

"Well, Kai, they'd be crazy not to. You'll love it here."

* * *

Two blocks from the wooden boardwalk that separated the beach from the town, The Sound Café looked fresh out of a travel magazine. The three rectangular windows were covered

TWO: KAI

by dark green awnings, a perfect contrast to the four oversized white umbrellas that sat over the cast iron tables. Each glass top table displayed a vase of fresh summer flowers. The matching chairs were an intricate pattern of sparrows sculpted from metal rods. Above the antique wooden door with two slivers of faded tinted glass, was a hand-painted sign with a scripted font that read, *The Sound Café.*

The black metal bell hanging over the door, announcing patrons' arrival, rang and the barista waved me in.

"What can I get for ya, hon?" the friendly barista asked the moment I reached the counter. Her crimson red lipstick stood out from her pale skin. Her black tank top showed the impressive art on her arms. The colors were so vibrant, you couldn't help but admire the hummingbirds hovering over the colorful flower tattoos she had. She gave me the warmest smile after she plucked a pen from her bun. *Everyone on this island is really nice.*

"What do you recommend? I've never been here before." I beamed, returning her friendliness.

The person waiting in line behind me groaned. *Okay, maybe not everyone is nice.*

I was about to look back, but the barista started to give me the rundown of what's good to have.

"We make the best muffins, we have about twelve flavors, but you're a bit late," she explained before bending over to check the remaining selection, which by the looks of it were just plain bagels and a small variety of cookies. "We normally sell out by nine o'clock," she continued.

I checked the wall clock and I couldn't believe that it was a quarter past ten. My circadian rhythm was still on Hawai'i time which was three hours earlier than the local time. "I'll come back tomorrow then, will you be here?" I asked, trying to make friends.

"Oh, come on!" the voice behind me grumbled.

I turned, ready to give this guy a piece of my mind, and was met by muscle. The sexy man had his arms crossed, accentuating the biceps that rippled beneath his tight blue t-shirt. His jawline was covered by well-trimmed facial hair that matched the color of his brown and slightly wavy hair. Those red lips looked supple, luring me to kiss them. Truth be told, I'm a sucker for tall guys. He easily had at least six inches on my five-foot-ten frame. He was wearing tinted sunglasses so I wasn't able to see his eyes, but I couldn't miss the scowl on his face. I hated to admit it was a sexy scowl.

The sexy-cranky man motioned to the cash register. Speechless, I let him go by.

"Hi Andrea, you got my order?" the sexy-cranky-gorgeous man asked the barista who went by Andrea.

"Sure thing, babe," she responded, and I was a little dismayed that she didn't call him by his name. I didn't know why I wanted to know either.

The sexy-cranky-gorgeous-suave man moved with precision, swiping his card while maneuvering a pink box in one hand with two to-go cups in a cupboard drink carrier stacked on top. I watched him curiously and when he turned around to leave, all I could do was smile. He froze for a few seconds while staring back at me.

"So, you're the reason why they're out of muffins," I joked, trying to lighten the mood. Because as much as this man annoyed me, I didn't want to make enemies.

But the stranger didn't crack. Nope. All I got out of him was a quick once over before he headed toward the door. *Jesus.* I watched him disappear.

I returned my attention to Andrea and let her know that I would be back earlier tomorrow to try their famous muffins. "My name is Kai by the way," I introduced myself and offered her my hand.

"It's Andrea," she smiled and accepted my handshake. "I'll see you early tomorrow!" she called out before I was out of the café.

On the street, I looked both ways, but the man had disappeared. I couldn't decide whether I was relieved or disappointed.

Three: Wyatt

Secret Knight

There were few things in life I hated more than being late. Thanks to that chatty tourist who spent ten minutes asking questions about those damned muffins, I wasn't just late, I was very late. *Man, that guy. Who smiles at a stranger? What the hell was up with that?*

Whatever.

I parked my red Chevy truck a block from the office and grabbed the box of muffins I'd ordered ahead of time because I knew how quickly they sold out, especially during summer.

Three doors past our waterfront office, I stopped by a manicured lawn that led up to a one-story grey bungalow. The house had a maroon door surrounded by flower beds full of red geraniums, the pink dogwood trees were in full display. I used the vintage brass door knocker to call and after two knocks, Mrs. Turnley answered.

"Coming!" she called. Seconds later, the door opened. "Hi sweety, how are you?" She opened the door wide and hugged me. Even though I'd expected the gesture, it still caught me by surprise. My body tensed, making me uneasy. After

THREE: WYATT

Afghanistan, I always felt uncomfortable with any level of affection.

"I'm sorry I'm a few minutes late. The café was busy with tourists. I got your muffins for your old lady's brunch."

"Thank you, let me grab my wallet."

"You don't need to pay me."

"Oh, Wyatt, you're gonna have to let me pay you sometimes. You do this for me every month."

"You know I don't mind, besides the café is about a mile from here and you don't drive."

Her eyes welled up and her features softened. "I don't know what I would do without you and Avery. Especially you. Do you have to sail today? Do you wanna come in for a few minutes?" Her eyes were pleading.

"I have a few minutes."

Her usual smile was back. She rubbed my arms as she showed me in.

Mrs. Turnley went to her kitchen with the box of baked goods while I stood in the living room and looked around. It felt like time stood still in her home.

Everything inside was original to the era of the home albeit in great condition. A testament to how this home was cherished. The brick fireplace with a wooden mantle was decorated with framed black and white pictures of Mrs. Turnley and her late husband George.

Some shots were taken from various vacations they had taken during a different time in their lives together. But one that stood out among the group was their wedding photo. Mr. and Mrs. Turney were a striking couple. She had the classic sixties look, mod hairstyle with a wide white headband and exaggerated upper and lower eyelashes, while Mr. Turnley stood proud with his suit that looked tailor-fit for his lean, but muscular physique.

"That was the happiest day of our lives," she said behind me, holding two glasses of iced tea. She handed one to me and motioned for me to sit down on the sofa or the matching striped chairs. I decided on the sofa with the brown crocheted blanket draped over the back. She handed me a white ceramic coaster with a blue anchor printed on it. "He was so nervous that day, he was just drafted in the military the week prior and scheduled to leave a few days later." She grabbed another framed picture of her husband from the side table and absently traced his image with her fingers. "He was different after he came back, he was easily agitated, tense all the time. But little by little it got better. It took months, perhaps years, but I got my George back."

I shifted uncomfortably in my seat, speechless. Her message was received. If only I was that lucky.

"Thank you, Wyatt, and not just for today, for everything."

"You're welcome, you know how to reach me if you need anything." It was getting harder and harder to concentrate.

"You're a good man. George had always thought you were one of the best kids out there. You marines stick together."

Drinking the iced tea for something to do, I tried to stay present. She was just being kind, but anxiety was dragging me back into dark places. "We do," I murmured after I cleared my throat. I needed to get out of there. "I should get going," I stressed before draining my glass because I didn't want to be rude.

I said goodbye to Mrs. Turnley and walked to our office which was adjacent to a wooden dock where our boats were moored.

THREE: WYATT

Lately, the *San Juan Winds* had monopolized most of my time. It was a whale watching and interisland cruise business that I built with my best friend Avery and his wife Elizabeth. Avery and I had known each other since we were in middle school. Our parents were best friends and because each of us was an only child, we developed a brotherhood that was stronger than any relationship I could ever remember. We had been through a lot of things together; from his father's failed battle with cancer, my parent's divorce, and my mom's death.

I was his best man when he married his childhood sweetheart, Elizabeth, a year after our high school graduation. He was the first person I opened up to about my sexuality. I thought being gay would change the dynamics of our friendship, but I was completely wrong. He had been the support I needed when my own father kicked me out of the house for coming out.

We joined the United States Marine Corps together right after college because we wanted to be part of something bigger for our country. It was a decision we didn't take lightly since his son, Elijah, had just turned one. I made it my mission to keep him safe for his family. Because unlike me, he had someone waiting for his return. That mission became harder to fulfill when they separated our brigade. Sometimes, it took weeks before we heard from each other and those were the longest weeks of my life; especially when news of fallen soldiers made its way to our barracks. The only time I was thankful for being separated from him was on the day of the ambush that took dozens of our comrades.

We were discharged almost at the same time four years ago. Although it felt like it was only Avery who came back from the war. The Wyatt who returned looked like me, sounded like me, but felt like a shell of a man.

Without anything else inspiring going for me, our business was something that I was proud of for several reasons. First, it had given me an outlet to focus my time and attention, so I didn't wallow at home with my self-destructive thoughts. Secondly, it had given me purpose to go outside and engage with others when all I wanted to do was curl on the floor and let the days pass me by. And finally, it had given me the motivation to stop counting down days but let those days count. These reasons might not seem much to some but those were the things that differentiated the barely walking and breathing version of me to someone who resembled the living.

It wasn't always easy. Hell, there were days when I questioned my sanity for starting something so out of my league. But with Avery and Elizabeth's help, it'd been as smooth sailing as a cruise on a calm summer's day. That was why I still felt guilty whenever I had to miss work because of the affliction I struggled to control. I was thankful that my last breakdown happened before my scheduled days off, so I only had to inconvenience Avery for a day.

Elizabeth was working on her computer with soft music by Adele playing in the background. "Mrs. Turnley?" she asked when I handed her coffee. She was perhaps wondering why I was almost an hour late.

I turned on my computer before answering. "Yup, she just needed to talk. You might want to warm that up." I motioned to the cup of coffee that had been sitting in my truck.

"That's sweet what you're doing for her. How long has it been since Mr. Turnley died?"

"It will be two years next month," I confirmed. "You and Avery do the same," I deflected the attention away from me.

THREE: WYATT

And that was the truth, the three of us had been there for Mrs. Turnley since she didn't have any kids and all her relatives lived in Seattle. "Have you confirmed the fishing group?"

Elizabeth nodded, her auburn hair bouncing on her shoulders. "Yes, they're arriving on the eighteenth. That's the week we're moving to our new place, so you'll be sailing with them."

"That's fine, does that mean I am off the hook for helping you guys move?"

"Nice try, you'll be done with them before we even get started. By the way, you're sailing with Roy," she continued.

"What? That man is so unreliable," I groaned. "What about those three high school kids we hired for the summer?"

"I know, but we're running on a skeleton crew that week. And the high school kids are camping that weekend. I can call and see if we can move it to a different day."

"No, it'll be fine."

Elizabeth's eyes were still on me and I had a decent guess why. I hadn't seen her since my attack and I never called to explain either. "What?" I exhaled, dreading the day already.

"Wanna talk about your emergency a few days ago?"

"Not even a little." I stood up and marched to the kitchen to warm up my coffee.

"You know that we're here for you, right?" she called out after me.

I knew that. I knew that they'd do anything for me, and it wasn't like I wanted to hide it from them. I didn't want my dark cloud to hang over them and I didn't want them to look at me differently. I didn't need them to remind me how broken I was. I saw that every day when I looked in the mirror.

Four: Kai

Vintage Red Chevy Pickup

The nightstand rattled when my phone vibrated, and an incoming call notification lit up the black screen. It stopped after a minute only to have another one follow and just like the first one, I ignored it and let it go to voicemail along with the rest of the messages that had been sitting there these past few days. I knew that after the second attempt, a text would follow, a routine that had started since I left Hawai'i. True to form, a succession of short vibrations buzzed against the shiny wood surface.

Pinching the bridge of my nose, I reached over to grab my cell and stared at the screen. My heart raced while my stomach dropped as it always did every morning, day after day. It used to be accompanied by the urge to vomit, so two out of three was an improvement.

Ma: I'll call you every day until you pick up.
Ma: We love you and we miss you.
Ma: Call us.

I deleted the messages and placed my phone on my chest. I stared at the abyss while I ran my other hand over the scar

FOUR: KAI

that etched from the crease of my elbow down to the middle of my forehand. My wounds had healed but the scars it left ran deeper than the cut. *I'm sorry, Ma.*

I plastered a smile on my face when I entered The Sound Café and immediately was welcomed by the scent of freshly baked bread and brewed coffee. The sounds of the machine steaming milk and the opening and closing of the old-fashioned cash register were accompanied by the soft music playing on the surround system. This place was so cool without even trying.

"Hi Kai!" Andrea greeted me after the bell announced my presence. "You came early and you just missed the rush. We've been busy since we opened." She draped the white kitchen towel she'd been using on her shoulder, glancing at the display shelves on her way to the cash register.

"I was afraid you'd run out. What should I get?"

"Let's get you started with our lemon yogurt blueberry muffin." She grabbed the pencil tucked in her ear this time since she wasn't sporting the same bun from the day prior and used the eraser end to push around metallic buttons.

"Wow, that sounds good." My mouth watered with the mere mention of the flavor combo.

"Because it is, it's one of our signature flavors. Coffee?"

"I'll have a mocha, please."

"You got it. Go ahead and find a place to sit, I'll bring 'em to you," she instructed me after I paid.

I chose the table toward the back and grabbed the seat facing the entrance. My head was trained on the door, like Pavlov's dog, whenever the bell rang. Three guys, probably in their teens, came in laughing and teasing as they entered the café.

What are these kids doing here at seven o'clock in the morning during summer break? They couldn't possibly be tourists the way they interacted with Andrea.

"Who is the unfortunate captain you troublemakers are sailing with?" Andrea asked and handed them three pink boxes.

"We're sailing with Avery today," the kid wearing a white hat with *The San Juan Winds* logo on it answered.

"Smells good," the other kid said after opening one of the boxes, taking a whiff of what was inside. "Do you think they'll notice if one of these muffins is missing?"

The third kid who wore glasses, the quieter one, was about to say something when the doorbell rang and there he was. The cranky guy from yesterday. Without sunglasses, I was surprised by the sweetness of his face and the sadness in his grey eyes. He looked vulnerable somehow. "Have you guys had breakfast?" he asked the group.

They all looked at each other before the kid with glasses answered, "We haven't. We're just picking these up for Avery."

"Hi Andrea, get these guys what they want and put the rest of the order on this," he said after handing her his credit card.

"Score," the kid holding the pink boxes exclaimed.

"Thanks, boss!" one of the rowdy kids said afterward.

He must be the other captain Andrea mentioned. *So not a jerk all the time.*

He turned then, and our eyes met. He stared at me for a good ten seconds before Andrea handed him his card back. "Why don't you guys finish your breakfast, and I'll drop this off," he said.

"You sure?" the kid holding the boxes hesitated, but eventually handed them over.

The man nodded.

FOUR: KAI

The three musketeers grabbed the closest spot to the cash register and continued ribbing each other.

The man, now holding three pink boxes that looked small compared to his muscular arms which had veins running along them, stood in front of the display case looking unsure. The slight discomfort on his face was kind of endearing, and without his aggressive demeanor, I finally saw how utterly gorgeous he was. My stomach fluttered when he turned toward me once more, his piercing grey eyes boring a hole into my soul.

I gave him a smile and a wave.

That seemed to rattle him. He looked away and dashed out of the café. He hopped into a pristine vintage Chevy pickup. The shiny red truck had a chrome front bumper that matched all the side mirrors and wheels. His hands were placed on the steering wheel and he looked back in my direction before starting his ignition and driving off.

Well, that was interesting.

Five: Wyatt

Fourth of July

I needed to be home before the craziness that was the Fourth of July started. Drunk Islanders and tourists flooded the streets, vying for the best spot to watch an overrated firework display year after year. I haven't seen it since high school and I have no desire to suffer through it ever again.

I grabbed my headphones out of my pocket and placed them on my desk next to Elijah's picture so I'd be ready when the fireworks show started. Drowning the loud explosion with music had kept my attacks at bay these past few years.

"I hate monthly reports," Avery moaned, looking at the receipts scattered around his desk while holding a steaming cup of coffee in his hand. His eyes were red from staring at his computer monitor.

"We'd finish early if you'd stop whining," I said, my focus never leaving the spreadsheet in front of me, matching every transaction line by line from the previous month. "And you say that *every* month. Besides, I told you I could do it myself." And that was the truth. I didn't mind working on holidays

FIVE: WYATT

since it meant no interruptions from anyone and I could do the task alone. Perhaps faster.

"Dude, it's Fourth of July, I wasn't about to let you do this on your own. This is our business," Avery explained while rubbing his neck with his other hand. "I need to be outta here before it gets dark though. I want to see the fireworks."

I huffed out a breath and shook my head at his last statement. I didn't get it, walking around bumping into people. *No, thanks.* I had zero tolerance for crazy, especially when I had tasks that needed to be done, *or ever—*

"What?" Avery asked, crossing his arms and leaning back in his chair. "You're the grumpiest fucker on this island, you know that?"

"Oh Geez, that just broke my heart," I mocked, placing both my hands over my heart. "How could I possibly sleep at night thinking that?"

"You're something else."

"Yup, now can we focus?"

We clicked and typed away for the next couple of hours.

"Alright buddy, you're on your own. Elizabeth is waiting for me by the boardwalk." Avery said, taking me out of my zone. He was standing by the door, his computer had been turned off and his pile of receipts was stacked neatly on his wooden desk. I hadn't even noticed him move.

I glanced at the time on my computer and was stunned that it was almost eight o'clock in the evening. My stomach growled loud enough for Avery to hear.

"Dude, get something to eat, will you?" he chuckled.

The mention of eating made me even hungrier and I grabbed a protein bar that I kept in my drawer.

"I meant real food. By the way," he hesitated with a smirk.

"I stopped by the café yesterday to pick up some coffee and Andrea said you've been there a couple of mornings in a row." His statement was disguised as a question.

"So?" I didn't have to look up to know that he was watching me. He's one of the most intuitive men I know. Not to mention nosy.

"You hate going there in the morning. That's why you always send us there to pick up our orders for the charter."

"I don't know what you're talking about. I've gone there in the morning," I said, pretending to work. "What?" I barked because I could feel his gaze still focused on me.

"Nothing, I'm just wondering is all," he said.

"Well, don't. The café is open for everyone, the last I checked." I immediately cursed myself for saying too much. This was Avery's modus operandi which tricked you into blabbing any secrets and intel.

He raised both his hands in surrender, but his smirk said otherwise. "Okay, I guess you better get back to work then."

"I never stopped," I murmured.

Avery shook his head and grabbed his car key, then headed out.

"Enjoy the crazies," I yelled before he was out of earshot.

I resumed working as soon as Avery left, clicking away on my keyboard and getting lost with the mission in front of me. Honestly, I enjoyed the silence and solitude that had become my simple sanctuary. All thoughts of cafés and a certain sparkling dimpled smile were pushed to the back of my mind. I was determined to stay focused on work, oblivious to the time as night fell.

FIVE: WYATT

The outside turned orange and red as if a fire was coming down from the sky. Vibrations started to rattle the windows of the office.

Boom!

A loud noise from the distance startled me, and in an instant, the room started to close in. Everything went dark and the sounds of boots pounding on the floor resonated into my surroundings, taking me back to the war zone.

Boom! Boom! Bang!

More explosions were followed by cries of help.

My heart started to race, my pulse pounding in every vein of my body.

"Ambush!" someone yelled.

Fight or flight mode kicked in and I got up from my chair and went under the desk for cover. I pulled my knees closer to my body and put my hands over my ears shaking my head frantically. My breathing became heavy, the forced sound of inhaling and exhaling cutting through the explosions. "It isn't real, it isn't real," I kept saying while I rocked my body back and forth.

"Wyatt, over here!" Martinez called.

"Jim?"

I leaned around my cover, searching for the source of his voice. "Jim, where are you?" I screamed.

Another explosion followed by more screaming. The sky was now covered with smoke, while red fire cut through the haze. Vibrations were harder and louder. Constant and never-ending.

"Lance Corporal, over here."

I patted my waist, searching for my weapon.

Nothing.

I looked around for my fellow soldiers, only to find that I was alone. The door vibrated some more, the knob rattled.

"Wyatt!" Martinez yelped. His voice came from the line of fire.

"I'm coming, Jim!"

The smell of sulfur suffocated me when I got outside. "Jim!" I yelled in between louder booms, their pounding matching mine. "Jim," I repeated when I didn't hear any response.

Boom!

Another loud explosion caused me to be off-balance. I landed on a hard surface, a dull ache knocking the wind out of me. I'm not very religious, but I prayed to anyone who'd listen to save Jim before our enemies got to him.

I stared at the red sky while more and more explosions followed. Fire blazed down from the sky before disappearing into acrid smoke. "Jim!" Wells of tears flowed down my cheeks.

Footsteps closed in. The Taliban had found me. I closed my eyes and thought about happy memories to take with me to the end, but nothing came. People said life flashes before you when facing the end, but sorrow and heartache were all I could remember. The vision of my mom succumbing to her battle with cancer, my dad throwing me out of the house, Jim's death, and the constant nightmares that never failed to visit.

"Are you okay?" someone said, the footsteps were louder, a voice became clearer. "Are you okay?" the voice repeated when I didn't reply.

Confused, I slowly opened my eyes.

It took a minute for my eyes to adjust, for my mind to return to the present, but when I did, a pair of familiar brown eyes greeted me. I didn't know what was more horrifying, the fact that I just broke down in public or the fact that the subject of

FIVE: WYATT

my every thought for the past few days was staring back at me after he just witnessed me crumble and fall apart.

Six: Kai

I've Never Seen a Sunrise

This was the first holiday that I didn't celebrate with my ohana and a small part of me longed for a chance to be with them. There weren't any passing days when I didn't think about them and when I did, the now-familiar stabbing pains in my chest always followed. I kept reminding myself that this was the price to pay for the fresh start I so craved.

* * *

The view of my ohana's house became smaller as I glanced at it from the passenger's side mirror of my cousin Mikaela's car. I wanted to see it before I left Oahu for good, to create a mental image in my head of those days that filled this home with happy memories. With a heavy heart, I opened the window to let fresh air in and blow away the remnants of tears that had been flowing down my cheeks since we'd gotten in the car.

SIX: KAI

The road was quiet this early in the morning. Palm trees swayed against the purple sky with faint twinkling stars that started to give way to the dawn.

"You sure 'bout this, ya?" she asked, dividing her attention between the road and me. "No one blames you for what happened. You know that, right?"

I took a deep intake of air and focused my sight on the Waimea Bay beach where I spent most of my days surfing and playing under the sun. The waves crashed against the shore as if calling my name one last time. I've never been away from home longer than the span of four weeks, and those four weeks I spent during my internship in Seattle were the loneliest times of my life.

"Kai! Are you listening?" she called out.

"Can you pull over?"

"What?" she asked, taken aback by my request.

"Can you pull over, please?" I pleaded.

Mikaela slowed down searching for a safe place to park.

I yanked the door open before she was even able to stop and I ran toward the beach. I kicked my shoes off, leaving them behind me. Hopping on one foot, I yanked off my socks so I could feel the soft grit of the warm sand caressing my soles one last time. My desperation kept me running toward the turquoise ocean waves even though my lungs ached with a sharp pain in my chest.

Mikaela had followed me, picking up my socks and shoes. She stayed on the beach watching me while I stood knee-deep in the waves. "I know they don't blame me," I yelled over the surf.

"Then, why are you doin' this?"

"Have you ever had someone look at you and feel that they wanted to say something, but they just don't know how? Or if they even should?" I turned and looked back at Mikaela when she didn't answer. "That's what I feel when I look at Ma and Pa. The guilt *that I feel knowing that I'm the one who put the stress on our ohana is more than I could bear."*

She wiped away her own tears as she let me continue.

"And that is why I need to leave, so I don't have to remind them of that." A strong wave pushed my weakened knees, causing me to fall and soaking my shorts.

* * *

I wanted to enjoy the festivities without being around a ton of people. After searching for a semi-quiet place, I found a dock that belonged to *The San Juan Winds*. It was a mile from Main Street where the firework display was happening. I'd seen this charter pass by every morning with loads of tourists hoping to get a glimpse of humpback and killer whales, or what locals called *Orcas*. I knew I wasn't supposed to be there, but it was open and everyone on this island was gathered by the waterfront for the Fourth of July show. Earlier, I saw big red, white, and blue fliers that advertised that it was going to be the year's biggest and loudest event.

So far, it was definitely proving to be the biggest and loudest.

The sky was filled with bursting red, yellow, and orange fire, accompanied by Katy Perry's song *Fireworks*. The light from the fireworks illuminated the calm water, making each burst magical. The boom and bangs of every colorful torpedo launched into the air were met with a roar from the crowd, and I couldn't help being happy for them, momentarily forgetting my loneliness.

"Jim," someone yelled from the small office building adjacent to the dock.

A silhouette of a man came out of the building, still yelling. He was frantically searching the area, looking for someone named Jim.

Another loud bang made him look up, causing him to lose balance and he fell on his back. Hard.

I sat and watched, waiting for him to get up. When he didn't, I got up to check that he was alright. "Are you okay?" I yelled hoping he'd hear me over the explosions that reverberated everywhere. I moved closer, not taking my eyes off of him. His whole body was trembling, and it couldn't possibly because he was cold. It had been one of the hottest nights since I'd arrived, and that was saying something coming from Hawai'i.

"I'm so sorry," the man kept repeating. Tears were reflecting the bursts of light from the firework while he sobbed, his chest shuddered.

The closer I got to him, the more familiar he looked, and realization dawned on me when I was standing above him. This man was the reason why I went to the café every morning, hoping to get a glimpse of his handsome face.

My heart broke for him. He was in distress and I had no clue what to do. I couldn't leave him, I knew that much. "Are you okay?" I asked once again.

He slowly opened his eyes and they stared at me with confusion. Beads of sweat formed on his forehead, plastering his brown hair to his temples in dark soaked locks. He was breathing through his mouth. He looked toward where I came from, immediately bringing his eyes back to mine. His hands were balled into fists, but he didn't look violent or aggressive. He looked scared.

I kneeled and his eyes became a fierce, stormy grey watching my every move.

He sat up and abruptly scooted away from me.

I raised my hands and spoke softly. "I just want to make sure you're okay. You hit your head pretty hard there." I showed him the fronts and backs of my hands, proving my intentions were safe.

I switched from my kneeling position and crossed my legs to sit. His grey t-shirt was soaked with sweat and I couldn't help but notice the chain hanging from his neck with two tags on it. He must have seen me trying to read the writing on them because he quickly tucked them inside his shirt.

I looked up as the sky exploded with color for the big finale. It was incredible. Blue, red and white sparks bursting against the black canvas. Next to me, the man wailed, and when I looked back down, he was cowering, hands covering his ears and head tucked between his legs.

"This is not real, this is not real, this is not real," he whispered. It was clear the noise was triggering for him. With his current state and the ID tags around his neck, I had a decent guess as to what that trauma was.

"Hey, you're fine. It's just the fireworks. See, look up, they're just fireworks."

He was rocking himself. "They're not here. It's not real."

"You're right, they're not here. It's just you and me, no one else," I assured him.

His rocking slowed and he lifted his eyes to mine. His eyelashes were soaked and his eyebrows dripped with sweat. He was weary, looking around us, staring at the now pitch-black water and back to the building he'd exited earlier.

"No one will hurt you," I said with conviction.

He looked me straight in the eyes, undeniable fear in them.

SIX: KAI

I decided that I wouldn't leave until he did. "Is there someone I can call for you?"

He averted his eyes from me and stared at the planks of the dock.

"Is it okay if I stay?"

He didn't say anything.

Deciding that his silence was consent, I hunkered down to stay for as long as he needed me.

Minutes became hours and not a single word was uttered between him and me. The inky night sky gave way to the grey lavender dawn. One glance at the stranger next to me confirmed that the dark clouds which had taunted him during the fireworks show were still there. He was staring at the horizon lost in thought. Watching him from my angle while the sun rose gave me a better vantage point to study his face. With the golden highlights, he was breathtakingly handsome in a rugged kind of way. His left eyebrow had a small cut that made him even sexier. His arms, which were resting on top of his knees pulled toward his body, were muscular even when relaxed. The tight shirt he was wearing did nothing to hide his impressive sculpted shoulders from bursting out of their confinement. My eyes landed on his stomach and wondered exactly how many packs were in there.

He glanced over and caught me studying him. My face burned from embarrassment, but if he was mad about my perusal, he didn't show it. In fact, he laid back on the dock propping himself up with both of his elbows. "I've never..." His voice cracked, a little gravely from not speaking for hours. He cleared his throat and continued, "I've never seen a sunrise before."

I could listen to him speak all day. His baritone voice was

thick and the fear in his voice from last night was gone. With my eyes still trained on him, I replied, "Didn't you get up early in the military?"

His brows furrowed and confusion etched his features. "How did you know I was in the military?"

I hesitated for a moment before reaching over to pull the chain from under his t-shirt. He followed my every move. My fingers brushed over his warm skin near his collarbone and I didn't miss the slight shiver and gasp he released when we connected. Feeling bolder than I'd ever been, I held the tag between my index finger and my thumb, showing it to him. "This was hanging out last night and I just assumed that you were," I explained. He didn't say anything for a while and self-conscious by my quick assumption, I laid back on the wooden dock and stared up at the yellow and blue sky.

He rolled to his right side to face me and propped his head up with his right arm. "Morning is just something that tells time, you know. I've never really watched a sunrise." He looked down at me, his eyes meeting mine.

I watched his lips move as he spoke, and I could've sworn he was staring at mine too.

"Wyatt Miller, I was with the Marines," he reached with a free hand to shake mine.

I looked at his hand for a split second and noticed scars. "Nice to meet you, Wyatt. My name is Kai Lobo." I shook his hand and was taken aback by the strong grip and the way his touch sent tremors to my spine. I gave him my best smile which was met with a smirk that almost looked like a smile. "Was?"

"Yeah, that was a few years ago," he quipped, evading my question. "Kai," he said my name as if it was a question once

SIX: KAI

he took his hand back.

The sound of my name on his lips made me say prayers to all the deities out there. *Please, please be gay.*

"That's a cool name," he continued. I was a little disappointed when he laid on his back and stared at the sky that was bluer than earlier.

"It means water in Hawaiian," I explained as I memorized everything about him. He had the most striking grey eyes that unfortunately matched the stormy clouds that had been hanging over him since we'd met. "My mom and dad gave me that name because I was born in February. You know Aquarius and all." I was unable to stop the sigh with the mention of my parents.

Wyatt glanced at me from the corner of his eye, but he didn't say anything. I didn't know what it was about him that made me want to tell him everything. I was a chatterbox, no doubt about that, but not when it came to my personal life, a subject that I could dodge with ease. Maybe because I knew deep inside that I would have to initiate all the talking with him.

"That's very cool. Are you from Hawai'i?"

"Born and raised."

We stayed in silence for a while until the morning sun made its appearance. Wyatt got up and stretched his neck left and right then reached over to help me get up. The same shiver of excitement came back once our hands touched. His strong grip was something that I could get used to.

"Thank you for last night," he whispered.

"You're welcome. I'm glad I was there," I said while trying to figure out what to do next. We were standing face to face, a couple of feet away from each other. He hadn't made the move to escape and I didn't want this moment to end. "Do you want to get a cup of coffee?" I asked, praying once again that he'd say yes.

I must have shocked him with my boldness because he raised an eyebrow and asked, "What?"

"Wanna grab a cup of coffee?" I repeated. "I found this great place a few days ago and they make the best coffee and muffins I've ever had. Maybe you've seen me there?" I joked, trying to sound as casual as possible. *Gosh, what was I thinking asking a stranger, a man nonetheless, for a coffee after his breakdown?* I felt like a fool.

"No, I don't think so," he answered.

I didn't blame him. "Of course. Anyway, take care of yourself, Wyatt," I said and hurried away before I made a bigger fool out of myself. Wyatt hollered something, but I couldn't hear it with the thumping in my ears. Once I crossed the length of the dock, I looked back and saw Wyatt planted where I left him, watching me.

"I'm such an idiot!" I cursed myself as I entered my apartment after my all-nighter with the Marine. I finally had the courage to ask someone out and that someone turned out to be Wyatt. Probably a straight man who was all confused by my questions. My face was still warm from embarrassment.

I made my way to the kitchen to make a cup of coffee. I can't remember the last time I stayed up all night without the mention of a party or college exams. Still feeling awake, I'd decided to just stay up all day and sleep later. I made my way to the living room and sat down on the sofa to think about him. He was such a mystery. A beautiful, irresistible mystery I would now have to avoid forever thanks to my humiliating rejection. I just wished I had recorded his voice, so I could play the sound of my name coming out of his mouth over and over. *"Kai, that's a cool name."* Damn. I was in deep and I hadn't even dived in.

Seven: Wyatt

I've Been Looking For You

The look of disappointment on Kai's face when I'd said *no* to his invitation was still reeling in my head minutes after he'd left. The offer came out of nowhere, so my refusal sounded harsher than I intended it to be. He'd seen me rattled, witnessed my breakdown, and then pulled me back to reality before my episode turned into a full-blown attack, similar to the one I'd had over a week ago. I felt exposed, so I said *no*.

I should've gone with him. I really should've, especially now that I was feeling somewhat better, better than I'd ever been after an attack. It wasn't like he was asking for my kidney or something. It was just a cup of coffee for Christ's sake.

When I finally had my wits about me and realized how I sounded, I ran the stretch of the dock, trying to catch up to him, but it'd been too late. I looked toward the direction he went, but he was nowhere in sight.

Feeling my exhaustion taking every last drop of my energy, I hopped into my truck and decided to search for him. There were only three coffee shops in town, and they were a block

SEVEN: WYATT

away from each other. I parked equidistant from all of them and started my search at the Sound Café, figuring that'd be a good place to start since I'd seen him there a few times already.

"Good morning, Wyatt! You're up early today," Andrea greeted me after I walked in.

I nodded to acknowledge her and looked around to see if Kai was one of the patrons sitting at a table, but to my dismay, there were no signs of him.

"What can I get for you?" she asked.

"Nothing, just looking for someone," I said before I walked out of the café, hurrying to the next spot. She said goodbye and I waved my hand at her.

I jogged to the next location only to find out that it was closed. One glance at my watch let me know that it wasn't even six o'clock in the morning yet. That left me with the last place, *Starbucks*. I groaned.

This establishment was the busiest. Most customers were tourists since locals avoided this place like the plague. The line at the cashier was already five people deep and almost every single table in the lobby was taken by ferry commuters and tourists waiting for their early morning whale watching tours.

I'd never been around this many people after one of my episodes. In fact, Kai was the first person to witness me break down in the middle of an attack. The crowded coffee shop threatened to pull me back to the battlefield, the one in my mind.

My breath started to get heavy and my hands became clammy. I fought the urge to run away and walked closer to the back of the store to check if Kai was there, but just like The Sound Café, he wasn't.

Suddenly feeling fatigued, my shoulders sagged, and I

headed toward the exit, bumping a distracted customer along the way.

"What the fuck dude?" he spat, giving me a death glare.

But I didn't care, I just needed to get out of there. I waved my apology then headed out. Once I got in my truck, my eyelids grew heavy and I began to doze off.

A continuous tapping on my window woke me and I found Avery looking in. I hadn't realized that I'd fallen asleep in my truck. Concern was written all over his face. I rolled my window down and the cool morning breeze coming from the water nearby, somehow sobered me.

"What's up?" I asked once the window was down, hoping to hide the unsteadiness of my voice.

"What are you doing here?" he said after looking in the bed of my truck. "You look like shit," he continued and reached over to touch the sleeve of my shirt. "And you're soaked."

I brushed his hand away from my shirt. "I'm fine. Will you let Elizabeth know that I'll be late today? I don't have any trips scheduled so it shouldn't be an issue."

"The fuck dude, what's wrong?"

Instead of answering, I jammed my keys into the ignition and my truck roared to life with a grumble. "I said I'm fine. I'll talk to you later."

"Wyatt!" he yelled while stepping back to let me drive away and looking perplexed at my behavior.

The following morning, after another successful charter, I started cleaning up the boat to make sure we'd be ready for

SEVEN: WYATT

the next sailing. It'd been great seeing the pod of Orcas minutes after we sailed. It was an amazing experience for our customers and even better for me. It meant not spending the entire morning looking for the elusive creatures, which allowed extra time to stop by the café and to check if Kai was there.

"I heard you saw a pod of Orcas this morning," Avery said after exiting the office and grabbing one of the hoses to power wash the deck of the boat, a routine we did after each sailing. I suspected that he wasn't there to help or chat about the Orcas, and my speculation was confirmed when he continued. "You still go to your appointments, right?" he inquired.

I pulled the rope attached to the boat and tied it on one of the hooks on our wooden dock, close to where Kai had last seen me. *What a way to meet. He probably thinks I'm some kind of loser who breaks down in public*, that thought made me cringe. I didn't know what about the last episode was different, but it was. Not better, not worse, just different.

"Wyatt," Avery called me back to the present.

"What?" I nearly barked. Chit-chat after sailing a boat load of talkative tourists, was the last thing I needed.

"Don't *what* me. What happened yesterday?" Avery's rapid firing of questions continued.

"Nothing happened."

"Bullshit! You fell asleep in your truck, wearing the same clothes you had from the night before."

"I just had another episode, but I'm fine now."

Avery studied me, not buying it. As much as I hated being interrogated, I knew that he only wanted to make sure I was alright. "We're here for you, man. We're family. Don't shut us out."

"I know… I'll be okay."

He dropped the subject and helped me finish cleaning the boat, then walked with me as we headed to our office. "Oh, before I forget, we've been meaning to ask you something."

Oh, what the fuck now? I held my breath for another onslaught of questions. "What?" I asked, gritting my teeth.

"Geez, you need another cup of coffee!" Avery chuckled.

"I've been trying to get out of here to get some, but you keep bugging me."

"Anyway, we're thinking if it's time to renovate our office. The business has been thriving since we added the fourth boat, and this old shack is showing its age," Avery explained.

It was a great idea. We'd been putting it off for months and investing in a remodel of our space was a smart business decision. "Let's update our software too, so I don't have to listen to you bitch about reports," I said.

"Terrific, we'll start looking for an architect and contractor. Elizabeth will go apeshit after I tell her you agreed."

"Okay, I've got to go!" I grabbed my truck keys and he didn't even wait for me to leave before calling his wife.

"Hey, babe—Elijah? Can you give the phone to mommy? Hey baby, Wyatt's on board. It took a lot of convincing, but he caved. You owe me big time."

I shook my head at his ridiculousness. I would never admit it, but I envied what Avery and Elizabeth had. *Only if I was that lucky.*

"If you're here for the muffins, we're sold out," Andrea greeted me when I walked into the café.

"It's okay," I said, looking around. The place was packed as

SEVEN: WYATT

usual, but the one person I wanted to see again was nowhere around. *I hope he didn't stop coming here so he could avoid me.*

I shook away the self-destructive thoughts and made my way out and instead of heading back to my truck, I decided to walk on the beach to get some fresh air, something that I rarely did. Ironic, since I practically lived on a boat.

The disappointment of not being able to see Kai diminished the closer I got to the beach. The sound of waves and the breeze coming from the water blowing on my face relaxed me and I thought about the number of times I used to spend on this boardwalk with Avery when we were thinking about what kind of business to open together.

"Wyatt?"

Goosebumps erupted over my entire body after hearing my name. I knew who it was before turning to where it came from. *Kai.*

He was sitting on one of the pieces of driftwood resting on the shore and he stood up when he saw me walking toward him, uncertainty on his face.

"Hi," Kai said, looking down at his feet playing with a small rock on the beach, his hands tucked into his pockets when I reached him.

"I'm sorry—" I was interrupted by a group of screeching seagulls passing by, screaming *ha-ha-ha* loud enough to drown my voice.

"What?" Kai asked before leaning closer.

"I'm sorry for turning down your invitation?" I continued.

His eyes furrowed in confusion. "You are? Why?"

Flabbergasted. I searched for the best things to say but nothing came out.

Kai looked at me expecting an answer. The wind blew his

hair, partially covering his forehead, and the urge to touch him and put it back in place felt foreign.

The longer I stayed quiet, the higher the tension got. "Wanna have some coffee? I know a great place. You might have seen me there once… or four times?" Surprised at my attempt to land a joke, I shoved a hand through my hair and tried not to grimace.

Kai was unable to hide his smirk and the harder he tried, the more the dimples on his cheeks deepened. The most kissable red lips parted and his face brightened. "You know, they'll be out of muffins, right?"

God, he's gorgeous.

Eight: Kai

Even His Coffee Selection Would Be Sexy

My curiosity grew the closer we got to the café. With my mind going a million miles per hour, I stayed collected and tried not to be bothered by his intoxicating smell that was carried by the breeze. I ignored the way my stomach flipped whenever I got a whiff of the fresh scent that reminded me of the ocean breeze in Hawai'i.

Still puzzled, I stole a glance at him and if his tensed jaw and rigid posture were any indications, he clearly didn't want to be there with me. *How could someone be that wound up? Is this a date? Are we friends now?*

"Hi Wyatt," a cheerful older woman greeted before hugging him.

Towering over her, Wyatt leaned to give her his best attempt at a hug, looking even more uncomfortable if that was possible. "Hi Mrs. Turnley, how did you get here?" he asked after the shortest embrace in the history of all embraces.

"My neighbor Marion is visiting her friend," she said and pointed to the building across the street, named the *Spring Hill Retirement Home*. "And asked if I wanted to tag along," she explained while looking between Wyatt and me.

When Wyatt, who I was learning was a man of few words, didn't say anything after a few seconds, Mrs. Turnley reached out a hand to introduce herself. "Hi sweetie, my name is Anna Turnley."

"Oh, I'm sorry, this is Kai," Wyatt introduced me before I had the chance to respond to her. "Kai, this is Mrs. Turnley."

"It's nice to meet you, Mrs. Turnley."

"You too, sweetie. I haven't seen you here before, are you visiting?" she asked after shaking my hand.

"No, I just moved here recently."

"Oh, that's nice. Welcome to San Juan Island!" she enthused with sparkling eyes.

I returned her smile. "Thanks."

"You'll love it here. How do you know Wyatt?" she asked, followed by another glance between me and him.

"We just met a couple of days ago," I spoke first.

"We're just about to get some coffee," Wyatt continued.

"Oh!" Her smile grew wider with her eyes still sparkling, before she continued, "Move along then. Don't let me interrupt you, boys." The not-so-subtle wink she gave Wyatt made him shake his head, but that was the extent of his reaction. Mrs. Turnley waved goodbye before crossing the street to meet up with her friend.

"She's sweet," I said once we continued our walk to the café.

"She is," he agreed.

Like I said, a man of few words.

"Wanna sit outside?" he asked as soon as we reached the shop.

"Sure!"

"Why don't you grab a table and I'll get the drinks," Wyatt

EIGHT: KAI

said before he turned and headed in. The way he strode across the patio made me think a door was unnecessary, he could simply bust through the walls. The door opened and out came a couple holding their drinks. Instead of grabbing the door handle, he reached above their heads to open it, exposing a sliver of his tight abdomen, and making my breath hitch.

"Wait," I called out when I recovered from my shameless ogling, but he was already inside. I was about to follow him to let him know what I wanted to drink, but a group of teenagers tried to take our spot. "I'm sorry, but I'm actually sitting there." Expecting a smart assed comment or a rude reaction, I braced myself for what was to come.

"Oh no worries, we'll find another one. Enjoy your day," one of them said, smiling.

I was both surprised and guilty for prejudging the kids. And I shouldn't be calling them kids, I was only twenty-four years old and these guys were probably just a few years younger than me.

After reclaiming our spot, I looked around and marveled at the quaintness of this small town on this beautiful island. The streets were lined with a clash of classic, art deco, and contemporary buildings that somehow found harmony with each other. The blending of period styles reminded me of the project I presented before graduating from the University of Hawai'i's School of Architecture. Boutique shops ranging from small leather goods to old-fashioned candy stores lined Main Street. Each street had tall, black, ornate, metal street lamps that had an assortment of purple, red, and pink flower baskets hanging from them.

Wyatt came out holding a tray with four beverages and several cookies. Confused, I asked, "Is someone else joining us?"

Wyatt combed the back of his head and looked at me sheepishly. "I forgot to ask what you wanted so I ordered a latte, an iced coffee, a mocha, and a plain black coffee," he said. "Same with the cookies." He pointed to each one of them and gave me the rundown of their flavors. "This is chocolate chip," he said when he pointed to the one on the right. His finger moved to the one in the middle, "This is white chocolate with coconut and macadamia nuts, I figured you might like that being from Hawai'i and all." Then he pointed to the one in the last cookie, "And this is oatmeal raisin if you're trying to be healthy. They're out of muffins and this is all Andrea had left. This place is very popular with tourists and locals so they're usually out of the good stuff around this time. But you already know that." He blew out a breath and leaned back in the metal chair, avoiding eye contact.

Speechless, the best I could do was listen to every single word that was coming out of his mouth. That was the most considerate and thoughtful thing someone outside my family had ever done for me. Not even my ex-boyfriend would've done that. I swallowed the bile creeping out of my throat at the thought of my ex-boyfriend, Noah. "Thank you. You could've just come out and asked so you didn't have to spend all that money," I said and pulled my wallet out of my pocket.

"What are you doing?"

"Paying some of this," I explained.

"I don't want your money. I invited you, so it's no big deal." He was rubbing his palm on his thigh, once again looking everywhere but at me.

"Which are you going to have?" I asked, my mouth watering, eager to try the cookies.

EIGHT: KAI

"Whatever you don't want," Wyatt answered.

I looked at him. *Didn't he know how incredibly thoughtful this was?* He hardly knew me and here he was putting me first and willing to sacrifice something just to make sure I got what I wanted. Maybe sacrifice was the wrong choice of words, but that's what it felt like.

"You don't want any of them?" he asked, after seconds of analyzing my slow decision-making.

"Oh no! I'd like the mocha to drink, and the white chocolate, coconut, macadamia cookie," I responded to avoid making a complete idiot of myself.

"Great choices," he said, as he grabbed the black coffee without putting any cream or sugar in the cup.

Of course, even his coffee selection would be sexy.

A few minutes had gone by and it quickly became obvious that Wyatt didn't want to start the conversation. I could end his misery by letting him off the hook or just leave, but there was something so intriguing about him that I couldn't pull myself away and I was determined to find out what that was.

Nine: Wyatt

Let's Start Over Again

I wanted the mocha, but because the universe had never been a fan of mine, it let Kai choose the drink that I wanted. The odd thing was, I wasn't bothered, not even a little. I could've easily come out and asked him how he liked his coffee, but the group of teenagers that came in would've hogged the line, and since Andrea had sold out of their muffins, the café's cookie collection was getting thin and I wanted Kai to try them all.

The uncomfortable silence between us was starting to gnaw at me. *Why do I have to be so awkward?* Feeling uneasy, I shifted in my seat and thought of ways to get a conversation going, but nothing came out. Instead, anxiety, panic, and nervousness heightened the prolonged silence, making every moment excruciating. Bullets of sweat began to form on my forehead while Kai studied me, a lazy smile on his dimpled face.

I thrived on silence, it'd been my comfort zone these past few years, but ironically, at this very moment, silence was the last thing I needed. It was a wonder I was able to secure a date

NINE: WYATT

in the past. If I'd met me, I wouldn't pick me either.

Moments passed without a single word being spoken. I considered having pity on Kai and letting him out of whatever this was so he could be on his merry way, but I wasn't willing to give up on this botched coffee date yet. It didn't escape me that Kai took his time sipping *my mocha*. I wasn't any better, I imitated his every move hoping to buy time and that he'd speak first.

We found ourselves in a staring duel and whenever he caught me staring at him, I forced myself to look away.

"Okay, it looks like we have two options here." Kai finally spoke. "We could call it, and pretend this awkward day never happened."

I held my breath, waiting for the other option and hoping that it didn't include parting ways and forgetting this day ever happened. As painful as this was, I wanted to be there with him, even if all we did was stare at each other. But I knew it wasn't fair to subject him to this social torture just because I wanted to be in his presence.

"Or..." he trailed off. "And I'm really hoping you pick this option." He held his hand up and crossed his middle and index fingers. "We can start over again and maybe, more talk, less awkward?" he finished, beaming.

And just like that, the tension in the air was defused by his charm. How could he turn the bad into something so hopeful, so easily? He was about to say something, but I cut him off and said, "I'll take the second option." Flustered by the excitement of knowing that he didn't want this day to end, just like I didn't.

"Great!" Kai's eyes widened, his face splitting from a breathtaking grin. "Wanna walk instead?"

"Yes," I agreed and if I was flustered then, I was a goner now.

His perfectly positioned dimples on each cheek and the way his light brown eyes dazzled with the sunlight reflecting through, made him irresistible. His red lips were accentuated by his tan complexion as if he were just coming from a long tropical vacation. Call me crazy but his skin actually glowed.

There was something about Kai that pulled me in, and I knew that it was more than just his striking good looks. I hadn't planned on walking along Main Street, but I couldn't seem to say *no* whenever he was around.

This had been a great idea. I don't know why I didn't spend more time out and about in our town. While we walked, I began to see things differently. The Victorian homes and sculptures from our local artists adorned Main Street of Friday Harbor. Our little town was charming. "Interesting."

"What is?" Kai asked, pulling me out of my new discovery.

"Huh?"

"What's interesting?"

I didn't realize that I'd said that out loud. "It's beautiful here," I shrugged.

"You're just now realizing that?" he mused.

"I've passed by this place hundreds of times. I've seen all this, but I've never *really* noticed it. Somehow, it's different," I explained.

"I get that. Sometimes, we don't appreciate the things we have until they're gone, or you're not there to see the beauty anymore." Kai took a sip of his drink and peered at the water. It was only there for a split second, but there was a flash of sadness in his eyes, and his voice cracked ever so slightly saying those words. He took a long breath and continued, "How long have you lived here?"

"I've lived here my entire life, except when I left for college

NINE: WYATT

and a two-year deployment in Afghanistan after that."

"Thank you for your service. This is truly a wonderful place. You're lucky to be surrounded by all this beauty."

We passed by the small park overlooking the Friday Harbor Marina and sat down on one of the wooden benches. The neighboring islands framed the glistening cold waters of Puget Sound as sailboats peppered the water with their bright colorful sails.

"Wyatt?" Kai asked.

"Yeah?"

"Can I ask you something personal? You don't have to answer if you're uncomfortable with it."

I was afraid this was about my breakdown and what brought it on.

There was a short pause before he continued. "Are you gay?"

Kai's question confused me, not because of the question itself but because I thought he already knew the answer. I'd never hidden my sexuality after coming out in my senior year of high school. Everyone in our small town knew who I was because I grew up here, but I'd forgotten he wasn't from around here.

Kai must've figured I was offended by his question when it took me a while to respond. The uneasiness in his eyes matched the jitters of his hand, which he quickly shoved into his pocket when he saw me glance at them. He looked so adorable chewing on his bottom lip between sips. Losing his patience, he asked, "Did I offend you?"

"Yes, I'm gay and I've been on my own ever since my old man kicked me out of the house."

"Okay, that's good news," he smiled. "Not the being kicked out of the house part, because that's awful, but the gay part," he mumbled. "I am too, but I think you got that, but then again I shouldn't just assume you do, you can't just assume that someone's gay," he paused, taking a breath. "Like, hello, who does that?" he continued and readjusted on the wooden bench facing the water, staring at the horizon. His face turned red and his hands shook a bit when he took another sip of his drink.

"Kai, it's okay. Breathe."

"Okay," he said and scooted closer.

"You're funny," I said, also scooting close enough for our hips to touch. I could hear my heart beating over the roar of Puget Sound and wondered if Kai could hear it too.

Ten: Kai

Wanna Go With Me?

I drowned my own guilt and the profound sadness that I felt after ignoring calls and texts from Ma every morning with the excitement of meeting Wyatt once again. I was giddy all day yesterday after learning that he was gay, but my heart broke for him after his declaration about his father. *His father* kicked him out of the house after coming out to him, the time when Wyatt needed the support of his family the most. It was another reminder of how fortunate I was to have loving parents. The support and unconditional love they'd given me when I came out were more than most people like me receive.

* * *

My legs were bouncing up and down, tapping on the wooden floor and scaring Cotton, our white West Highland Terrier. We named her Cotton because the color and fluff of her silky coat reminded us of clouds. With my clammy hands, I scrolled through my contacts to find Mikaela's number, then pressed call. "I don't know if I can do this," I said before she even had a chance to say hello, but she knew what I was talking about because I'd gone over the plan with her the night before.

"Why do you think dat is?" She answered, with a thick Pidgin accent from being born and raised in Hawai'i.

Worst-case scenarios ran through my head, the worst one being kicked out of the house or disowned. Where would I go? How was I going to survive? I was just sixteen years old. "What if they don't accept me? What if they kick me out?" *I asked her, my phone shaking against my cheek.*

"Kai, they love you and they're some of the most amazing people I know. They took me in and made me a part of your ohana when mom died, so I didn't have to go to foster care. Da Ma and Pa I know wouldn't do any of dat," she assured me. *"Wanna wait 'till I get home from picking Lei up?"* she asked.

As much as I wanted her support, I needed to do this alone. "No, I'll be fine. Listen, Ma and Pa just got home, I have to go," *I answered. The familiar sound of their car pulling into one of the carport spaces attached to our home made my heart pound even harder. Before I talked myself out of it, I got up, trained my eyes on the door, and watched it open as if life moved in slow motion.*

"Is everything okay, Kai?" Ma asked several minutes after I asked them to join me in the living room. She darted a worried glance at Pa. All three of us were sitting on the couch with me between them.

"Are you hurt?" Pa turned to ask, putting his hand on my back and rubbing it for comfort.

Moment of truth. I couldn't hide it anymore, not from the ones I loved.

"Ma, Pa, I'm gay," I said without hesitation. *I felt pride and relief from finally being able to say that out loud, but also scared beyond belief that my parents wouldn't accept my truth. I knew Mikaela*

TEN: KAI

was right about my parents, but I hated that there was a small part of me that doubted them. Fearing what I would see in their eyes, I leaned over and cradled my face in my hands. The tears had started to stream through my fingers, and run down my wrists and elbows.

Ma reached out, turning my head so she could see my face, hers was stained with mascara etching rivers along her cheekbones. "Don't cry, son. It's okay. We love you and nothing will ever change that. Always remember that," she assured me after kissing my forehead.

Pa scooted over and wrapped his arm around my back squeezing my shoulder. "We're so proud of you kid," he whispered.

"Are you guys okay with me being gay?"

"Why wouldn't we be?" Ma asked. "You're smart and kind. What more could any parent ask for?" she continued.

"Mahalo, Ma. Thanks, Pa" I said as I smiled at them, wiping my tears.

They wrapped me in their arms, and I'd never felt more loved.

The door opened and Leilani, my ten-year-old sister, came in followed by Mikaela who sported a big grin on her face. Lei was fresh from her ballet practice and was wearing a blush-colored bodice and tights with a dark pink tutu. My sister had shown potential since she was six years old and our neighbor, who owned a ballet school in town, had been helping her train to enhance her natural talent. "Why are you crying?" Lei asked Ma, before looking at me.

"Kai just shared something very special with me and your pa," she said, answering Lei's question.

"I just told them I'm gay," I continued, unsure how a ten-year-old's mind would process the news.

"Cool," she shrugged and waltzed toward us to give Ma, me, and Pa kisses.

"I'm so proud of you, Kai," Mikaela locked the door behind her before walking toward me. I got up to meet her halfway and gave her a hug. She'd been the first person I told about it, and the support and encouragement she'd given me fueled the fire in me to finally come out to my ma and pa. "Told ya," she teased.

* * *

I stared at the ocean feeling torn up inside because I missed my family and still regretted leaving the way I did when all they'd done was support me.

"Kai?"

I jumped when Wyatt said my name, turning my face away from him to subtly wipe my tears away, but I knew it had been too late. There was no way he didn't see them fall. I had been so deep in my memories, I didn't even notice he was there.

"Are you okay?" he asked with concern in his voice, and his stare was begging for an answer.

"Yes, I was just remembering something, but I'm fine," I mumbled and made space so he could sit down on the same park bench we were on yesterday. We had exchanged numbers and made plans to meet this morning. "Have a seat, I got your coffee," I said, handing him a black coffee just like he drank yesterday.

Wyatt sat down after grabbing the cup of coffee, his gaze still on me. Those stormy grey eyes still searched for an answer, but I wasn't about to burden him with my sob story. His face grimaced after taking the first sip and I wondered if I'd order the wrong drink. I couldn't have. I was positive that was what

TEN: KAI

he chose yesterday.

"Is that the wrong drink?" I asked.

"No, it's fine. I like it," he insisted. He leaned back and draped his muscular arm on the back of the wooden beach, occupying the entire length. I couldn't help but notice how big he was. "Sure you okay?" he asked. His clean scent was putting a spell on me once again.

"Yes, I am."

Wyatt just nodded and took another sip of his coffee.

Thankful that he stopped pressing me, I asked the question I forgot to ask when we were texting last night. "Do you work at night?"

"No, why do you think that?" The worry in his eyes was replaced with confusion.

"Well, you said in your text that this time was perfect because you'd be done with work," I explained.

"I work in the morning. I sail boats. Me, my best friend Avery, and his wife Elizabeth own The San Juan Winds." He paused for a second and looked out at a passing boat before continuing, "The dock where you saw me on the Fourth of July is where our office is located. I was in the middle of a monthly audit when you witnessed what happened."

That was the most information he'd shared with me since we met that night and not wanting to break the momentum, I let him continue.

"We own four boats. Two are catamarans for whale watching, and two are charter fishing boats for deep-sea fishing. Avery and I take turns sailing and we have few guys who help us on board. Elizabeth takes care of the catering and the bookings, but she hates paperwork so it's up to Avery and me to do the books."

"Wow, that's a lot of work... to do all that."

"It's not bad, all three of us work well together. What about you?"

"I'm an architect. I just graduated last year and I'm currently doing freelance work."

"Is that what brought you here?"

"Uh, yeah, you can say that." I cleared my throat and quickly changed the subject. "So, do you sail every day?"

"No, I try to take at least a couple of days off a week. Technically I'm off tomorrow, but offered to go to Westport to check out a boat that Avery saw online."

"I've heard about Westport. They're supposed to have one of the best spots for surfing in Washington." I couldn't help but smile thinking about waves and surfing. "The magazine I'd read said that surfs can get as high as eleven feet. Do you know how perfect that is?" I asked, my enthusiasm uncontained.

"I take it you surf?"

"I'm decent."

Wyatt was quiet for a while, mulling something over. "Wanna go with me?"

Eleven: Wyatt

San Juan, Portland, San Francisco

I didn't know where his mind was, but wherever it was, I disliked it already. The pain on Kai's face and the tears welling in his eyes set off something deep inside me. The need to shield him from anything that could cause him pain and harm was so foreign I didn't have adequate words to describe it. What I knew for certain was I wanted to do everything to make him smile.

He hadn't noticed me approaching and it took me getting closer to him before he heard me say his name for the second time, finally acknowledging my presence. Even then he'd choked on his words when he realized I was there.

"Are you sure I won't be a bother if I tag along?" Kai answered my invitation to join me with a question of his own.

He wouldn't be. Even if he were, I would have powered through it just to see that excited sparkle in his eye when he mentioned surfing. "Not at all." I took another sip of coffee and almost spit it out. I should tell him I hated black coffee, but I was a sucker trying to please him, so I pretended to enjoy it.

His eyes narrowed because he didn't miss my reaction to the

bitter drink. "Okay, as long as you're sure. It'll be nice to see that part of the state."

"Have you been anywhere since you arrived?" I asked as I watched his Adam's Apple bob after taking a sip of his drink.

"Just here. I mean, I've been to Seattle. I spent four weeks over there last year when I did my internship."

Places I wanted to take him, started flooding my brain even before he finished answering.

"How do you like it here?" I asked when we started walking to Kai's place. He wanted to show me where he lived so I could pick him up tomorrow morning for our trip to the coast.

"I'm enjoying it here. I love the setting and the people are very welcoming. I'm glad I came here first."

Curious about his last statement, I asked, "What do you mean, you're glad you came here first?"

"I couldn't decide where to live so I planned on staying in each city for a month before I settled on one, but I'm starting to love this town," he said as he waved to a couple of locals we passed.

"Where were the other places you considered?"

"San Francisco, Portland, and some others along the west coast. I can't live anywhere where it snows three months out of the year. I hate the cold," he chuckled.

"So, you only have a place to stay for a month?" I asked, surprised by my disappointment at hearing that.

"Yeah, but my landlord, Sam Matthews, told me I could sign a long-term lease if I decide to stay. Do you know her?"

I nodded. I was even more determined to make Kai love this place enough to stay.

It became my mission to convince him to stay.

"This is me," he said when we stopped by one of the single-

ELEVEN: WYATT

story homes a few blocks from the center of town. He wasn't too far from me and I could easily walk to his place. "I'd invite you in, but all I have right now is a couch and a bed."

I wanted to come in and spend more time with him, but it had been a while since I'd been with anyone and the mention of bed made my hands sweaty and my mouth dry. "So..." I cleared my throat, forgetting how to speak all of a sudden, "Pick you up at six?"

"Sounds good. Do you want me to pick up the coffee?"

"No," that sounded louder than I intended, but I didn't want him to get me another black coffee. "I mean, let's do it on our way out," I suggested.

"Okay, see you tomorrow," he said with a dimpled laugh.

Neither of us moved. There was a weird silence between us as I wasn't quite sure how to say goodbye. "Well... okay, I'll see you then." I waved, which felt real awkward given how close we were standing. I stumbled a bit as I turned back toward Main Street. *Way to go, Wyatt*, I chided. *Real fucking cool.*

Twelve: Kai

Let my Guard Down

Wyatt pulled his phone out for directions as soon as we passed the sign welcoming us to *Westport, Washington*, a quaint coastal town about a hundred and thirty miles southwest of Seattle and about two hundred miles from the San Juan Islands.

I rolled the windows down to let the fresh ocean breezes in. "I had no idea that it would take four hours to get here," I said while I took in the scenery. The terrain was flat, and we could see miles ahead. One side of the two-way streets was lined with rows of industrial fishing companies and the other side was filled with marinas storing boats of assorted types and sizes.

"Don't worry about it, I don't mind the drive," he said, glancing from the road and to his phone, following the map. "What's the name of the place again?" he asked.

"It's called Big Waves Surf Rental. I can look it up." I offered, so he could concentrate on driving. I googled the rental shop's address and hit directions to let Siri direct us to where we needed to go. "It's about two miles south from here."

Wyatt nodded since we were headed south.

TWELVE: KAI

A deer jumped into the road. Wyatt slammed on the brakes and the old truck skidded to a stop, his hand extending to hold me back in my seat.

I dropped my phone on the floor and shut my eyes.

Images of bright headlights flashed, followed by the deafening sound of a blaring horn and metal crunching surged from deep inside my memory bank. The blare of cries and sirens followed when I was hurled into the past. My vision was flooded with red and blue blinking lights and chattering voices came from the distance.

"We're okay, Kai," a disjointed voice said, but I feared opening my eyes knowing all too well the scene that would follow. "Kai," the voice repeated, softer and more familiar. A hand landed on my shoulder causing me to jump and open my eyes.

"Hey, we're okay. The deer's okay too. See, over there," he pointed toward a small herd of deer grazing on blackberry bushes, oblivious to what just happened. "That buck to the right came out of nowhere, but I was able to stop in time. I saw the signs about deer and elk crossings, so I've been on the lookout."

My heart was still racing, and I was only able to hear half of what Wyatt was saying. I grabbed my phone from the floorboard, and immediately it slipped away because of my shaking hands. Wyatt's eyes were watching me, and warmth spread all over my face from embarrassment. Just great. He's going to think I'm such a weirdo, freaking out because of a near accident with a crossing deer. I reached out to grab the phone once again, gripping the device tightly. "I'm sorry, that was silly," I blurted, forcing a laugh, a laugh too shaky to be convincing.

I took a deep breath before unlocking my phone to keep my

trembling body under control. He was about to say something, but a car behind us blew their horn, forcing him to turn his attention back to the road. I welcomed the interruption.

"In five hundred feet, turn right," Siri's voice broke the lingering silence.

"I think that's it, there to the right," Wyatt said, pointing to a small shack, painted purple with distressed surfboards nailed to the sides of it.

I checked my phone to see that he was correct, it was the surf shop and they looked like they were closed. "Are they open?" I asked. "The website says they open at ten." We left home at six, anticipating to arrive past ten in the morning, and we'd been on schedule even after stopping at the rest stop and getting gas. I checked my phone and then the dashboard of Wyatt's truck, and it was almost ten-thirty.

"Let me check it out," he said.

I released another unsteady breath as soon as he was out and stared at my trembling hands.

* * *

I landed on the floor, hitting the small wicker coffee table, causing it and its contents to flip and shatter onto the tile floor. Magazines scattered and the small ceramic turtle statue was in hundreds of sharp pieces. I pressed my fingers with my swelling lips and I tasted the iron of my blood. Shaking my head in disbelief, I hoped that what just happened wasn't real. But as much as I wanted to believe it wasn't, the proof was staring back at me. His six-foot-tall body towered over me, his face was contorted with fake remorse, and his

TWELVE: KAI

blue eyes were watery with plastic tears. I'd seen that look more times than I cared to count.

I loved him. That was the reason I stayed for as long as I did, but he had never laid his hands on me before. As I stared at him, I felt hollow. The love that I had for him was nowhere to be found. He had just knocked the last of my affection clear out of me.

If I hadn't lent Lei my Jeep, I would have just walked out. Even though it was storming, I had to ask her to come get me. I grabbed the phone out of my pocket and texted my younger sister.

'Please come get me,' the text read.

"I'm sorry, baby, I just got carried away. You know better than to provoke me when I'm having a bad day?" he shrugged, his insincerity was grating. Leave it to Noah to turn this around as if it was my fault that I was lying there, blood on my busted lips.

"You're kidding, right? I just fucking asked you why you were home this late," I fumed.

He shrugged. "I was with my buddies, my lieutenant gave me another demerit so we were just blowing off some steam."

"You couldn't pick up your phone to call or text?" I ignored his hand offering to help me stand up. His fist on my face would be the last time he'd ever touch me. I scrambled to my feet and ignored the glass pinching into my palm. "I should be the one you go to when shit happens. I'm your goddamn boyfriend," I yelled, pointing at him. I stepped back a couple of steps when he walked toward me, preparing myself for a possible second blow.

"Baby, relax I'm not going to hurt you," he took another step closer to me.

I moved back, putting my fists in front of me.

"Please, you think you can take me down? Give me a break," he mocked. "I went out with the guys because they know how my superiors have a hard-on for me. They're always waiting for me to

make mistakes. They're just jealous because I have the potential to be a SEAL."

That was the biggest crock of shit I'd ever heard in my entire life. "No, Noah. Your lieutenant isn't jealous of you. He doesn't give you demerits because he's picking on you. He's always on you because you're full of shit. You're never on time, you think training is all fun and games, and you aren't *fucking SEAL material." My extra emphasis on that last statement didn't go unnoticed.*

His nostrils flared, his blue eyes turning dark. The vein on his left temple was ready to pop at any moment when his fist balled up as he closed the distance between us. He grabbed me by the neck and pressed me against the wall.

I put all my energy into removing his hands from my neck. I was no match for Noah physically, but I wasn't about to go down without a fight. I pushed him away as hard as I could and moved behind the sofa as soon as I had him off me.

"Oh, you think you can take me down, Kai?" Noah walked slowly around the sofa and I moved in the opposite direction, avoiding him.

There's nothing I wanted more than to wipe that smirk off his face. I couldn't believe I stayed with him, but I thought he'd change. I thought that showing him how much I loved and cared about him would inspire Noah to be a better person.

I was so fucking wrong.

The storm outside had grown stronger. The thunder and lightning mirrored my emotions and the tension in the room was so thick I could choke on it.

"Kai," Leilani yelled from the door before she banged on it, her voice heard between claps of thunder.

"Oh, you called your little sister to save you?" he teased.

I ran to the door, to let Lei in.

TWELVE: KAI

"Kuya, what happened to you? Did that asshole do this?" she fumed, staring at my swollen, bloody lips. She stormed by me hell-bent on confronting Noah who was standing amidst the broken glass with his arms crossed. She was about to go after him, but I stopped her. Lei was a petite, but feisty girl. The exact opposite of the poise and control she showed on a ballet stage. She was one of the best ballerinas in Hawai'i and recently got invited to join the Juilliard School of Performing Arts for her senior year.

"Let's go, Lei. He's not worth it," I spat in his direction.

"I'm not taking you back if you walk out of here," Noah called after me, while I grabbed my wallet and keys from the kitchen counter.

"Don't worry, I have no intention of coming back. Let's go, Lei."

"What about your things?" she asked.

"There's nothing here worth keeping," I said while glaring at Noah.

We hurried toward my Jeep parked on the side of the curb. I felt surprisingly lighter. I needed that day to happen in order to wake me up from my fantasy.

* * *

Wyatt squeezed my shoulder to get my attention. His warmth brought me back from the past. "They're not open for another thirty minutes according to the sign. Why don't we get some breakfast while we wait?"

"Um, yeah," I said, staring at him, overwhelmed by all the emotions warring in my mind.

"Is everything okay? Sorry if that deer thing freaked you

out."

I got out of the car and walked side by side with Wyatt. "I'm okay. I'm just not a big fan of driving is all." And that was the truth, he didn't need to know why, and I was glad that he didn't push.

Wyatt kept glancing at me on our short walk to the diner, but I couldn't meet his eye. Instead, I let my head hang low, desperately trying to pull myself out of that horrific night.

Thirteen: Wyatt

Dance With Me?

"Are you sure you're fine?" I asked Kai one last time before heading over to check out the surfing equipment he'd reserved last night from the surf shop next door. He'd been quiet and a bit guarded since the abrupt stop to avoid hitting the deer. I couldn't get him to tell me why, but he'd been sulking ever since. He'd hardly spoken a word during breakfast. Odd considering he'd been the most talkative person I'd ever met in my life.

"Yeah, I'm fine," he shrugged.

I knew better than to push. He was hiding something for sure, but I'd be a hypocrite if I kept asking, something I wouldn't want anyone to do to me. Everyone was hiding something and whatever his demons were, I promised myself to never push him.

Just like the walk to the diner, we didn't utter a word to each other on our way to the surf shop which was a shame since I had high hopes for the day. I was hoping to get to know Kai better. I wanted to learn what made him laugh, what he liked, and what made him the happiest.

The automatic sensor attached to the store's door rang after

Kai opened it and I followed behind. No one greeted us once we got in, so we spent a couple of moments looking around the bright interior. The wooden floor squeaked with every step we took, and Kai looked at me and mouthed, *where is everyone?*

I shrugged my shoulders as if to say *I don't know.* I continued to look around and marvel at the selection of different surfboards.

"Those are called foamies," Kai said from behind me. His warm breath sent shivers to my core. "They're made out of foam. You notice how much bigger they are from…" he paused, looking around, "they're bigger than that kind." He pointed to a group of white surfboards with blue bottoms. "Those are called mini mal."

The way Kai talked about surfboards lit up his face like a kid in a toy shop. For Kai, these boards were invigorating. Thankful that he's finally starting to get out of the funk he was in, I asked, "Which ones are we going to rent?"

"Well, since you've never done any surfing before, we'll get you the foamie. It has better buoyancy, and it's wider. Perfect for beginners," he explained while examining each *foamie*, perhaps looking for something to hold my two hundred thirty pounds of awkward muscles. His eyes lit up and his lips curled into a smile when his attention landed on a rainbow-colored board. He pulled it out of the rail and handed it to me. "This is perfect!"

"Really?" I crossed my arms and met his eyes.

He tried his best to school his expression, but just like earlier, he hadn't been able to mask it. He burst into fits of laughter making his eyes glossy with tears. He was the most fascinating man I'd ever met. I've had boyfriends in the past. One was in high school and the other was in the military, but both

THIRTEEN: WYATT

relationships were hidden from the public. Not that I was in the closet or anything, but we didn't want to be the target of hate during deployment.

"What's so funny?" I pretended to be annoyed because unlike him, I'd been an expert at hiding and using a façade on demand.

"Nothing, I was just thinking how great you're going to look on this board while wearing a pink wetsuit?"

I grimaced. "I'd look hideous, people would laugh."

"I doubt anyone will give you a hard time with your death glares and hard muscles," he teased after squeezing my biceps. "Not with these guns."

I just shook my head, ignoring the effect his touch had on me. "Which one are you going to use?"

He grabbed my arm and led me to the other side of the store. "See those two boards with the very pointed tips?" he asked, pointing at two yellow surfboards with red trim about ten feet long. "Those are called gun surfboards. If we were on the North Shore of Hawai'i, I'd be using those. They're perfect for monster waves. But since we're not gonna be riding any *Jaws* today, I'll settle with these short boards, they're the fastest and the most responsive." He pulled a blue board from the rack and studied it front and back. "I can get to you faster just in case."

"In case of what?"

"In case of a shark attack," he winked.

The back door opened and the floor creaked when a young guy with long blonde hair greeted us with a big smile on his face. He was about my height with a slimmer build and was wearing a pair of board shorts under a white tank top which had a blue *Hang Loose* logo on the front. "Sorry about the wait, we're short-staffed today and I'm doing both the rentals and the instructions," he explained. "How can I help you guys?"

Kai extended his hand and spoke, "My name is Kai Lobo and I called last night about renting some boards and wetsuits."

The kid shook his hand and gave Kai the biggest smile, staring at him longer than I cared for. He was still holding his hand after a couple of shakes, so I extended mine to get his off of Kai's, and I may have given him a harder handshake than necessary. He seemed to get the point and put on his professional look once again.

Good.

"We'll take one of the foamies, one short board, the blue one over there, and two wetsuits, medium and..." Kai looked at me for my size.

"Extra-large please," I finished our order.

"And we won't need any instructions. I've surfed before."

"Oh, yeah? Where at, Kai?" the punk asked, angering me further by using Kai's first name.

"North Shore."

Punk's eyes lit up like a Christmas tree. "No way! That's dope."

Dope? Who the fuck still uses that word?

I glared at him one more time and when the kid glanced at me, he mellowed out and then moved back to finish our order.

Kai looked at me with a raised eyebrow.

I shrugged.

Whatever Kai was going through earlier seemed to have dissipated once we were near the water. He was back to my chatty Kai, who could charm the world with his dimples.

"Remember what I told you earlier? If you see a wave that you like, belly down, and paddle to it, and then hop up? It'll take a while before you get your balance, but once you do, it'll be

THIRTEEN: WYATT

worth it." He went around to check my back to make sure that I was all zipped up and the attentiveness and thoughtfulness made my chest tighten.

I've never had anyone care for me like him, not even my father. I sometimes wondered what it would have been like if my mom survived her battle with cancer. Would my life have been different? Would she have supported me when I came out?

"Ready?" Kai asked, staring at me with those warm caramel eyes.

"Yes."

Kai tapped my cheek and gave me a wink before turning to run the short distance to the shore and into the surf of breaking waves. He looked back to where I was planted. I was satisfied to just watch him put on a show, but he gave me the *Hang Loose* hand gesture before waving for me to join him in the water.

"Ready for another one?" Kai asked, minutes after the rest I'd recommended because we'd been swimming and riding the waves for two hours, in my case that meant standing up and face-planting from the board.

Sore from all the falls I'd taken on the water, I wanted to say *no*. But my mission included doing anything to keep him smiling and laughing. Plus, if I was honest with myself, I enjoyed his bright smile and the melody of his laughter. I wanted to be close to him. So, knowing that my twenty-eight-year-old body that felt like it was sixty would punish me later, I said, "Always."

"Awesome! I think I'm ready for the big one."

I knew he meant waves, but my mind wandered somewhere where it didn't belong. Once again I was thankful for the tight wetsuits we were wearing to keep us warm because it hid my growing erection. "Why don't you go ahead and show me how it's done? I'll take a video."

"Are you sure?"

"Absolutely." I pulled my cell from the waterproof case that came with the suit and got it ready to film Kai.

"Don't film my wipeouts, okay?" he warned, but the tone of his voice suggested otherwise.

"I won't make such a promise."

"That's okay. I don't wipe out," he winked and ran toward the water.

His cockiness only served to make him sexier.

Heading home, I should've been tired after our long day of driving, surfing, and checking out the boat Avery asked me to appraise, but I was fired up. The sun was just setting, giving a perfect view as we drove.

"Too bad that boat wasn't what you were looking for," Kai said, combing his hair with his fingers, his skin was rich like honey after playing on the beach for hours.

"Nah, we really didn't need another one, but Avery saw it online and thought it was a great deal."

"I'm still in awe about what the three of you accomplished." His compliment warmed my heart. I'd heard those words before from our neighbors and clients, but it felt different coming from him somehow.

"Thank you. It was tough at first, but with the three of us, we're managing just fine."

THIRTEEN: WYATT

Kai just nodded and returned his attention back to the road, the sea, and the setting sun.

"Do you have any other plans for the rest of the night?" My face warmed up as soon as the words came out of my mouth, but it'd been said so I decided to go for it. "I was wondering if you want to order pizza and have dinner with me? My place is coming up."

Kai was just looking at me, his expression not giving anything away. My pulse started rushing seconds after he hadn't replied. I was about to take my invitation back when he responded.

"Sure. Want me to call *Sopranos*?"

I blew out a shaky breath and just nodded, fearing my voice would give my excitement away.

"Hawaiian, okay? Or are you one of those pizza snobs who hate pineapple on their pizza?"

"I love Hawaiian," I blurted.

"They're the best," he teased and just like earlier, my mind wandered elsewhere.

I'd never been conscious of my home until Kai was in it. I looked around to make sure the place was presentable. Thankfully, I'd straightened up earlier, making sure everything was copacetic. Preferring to keep my house clean, my place looked like it always did, but I was hyper-critical because of my desire to impress the man standing next to me. My small, beachy home was the typical grey shingle-sided house that appeared all over the island. I kept my decorations minimal with grey furniture paired with whitewashed tables and bookshelves. I'd taken several photos of the boats and had them framed in whitewashed wooden frames. It wasn't much, but I got plenty of compliments on my simple yet stylish decor from Avery and Elizabeth. The furniture was also sturdy enough for Elijah to jump around whenever he visited. "Make yourself comfortable."

"Nice place, I love your framed photos. Did you take those?" Kai asked when he entered the living room.

"Yeah, I did over the past few years. I'm glad you like them."

"Who's the kid?" Kai asked, pointing to the only photo in my house that had people.

I couldn't stop my smile when I looked at me and Elijah sitting in one of our catamarans. "That's Avery's kid, Elijah."

"Oh," Kai smiled before moving along. He began checking my vinyl collection next to the record player I got from one of the garage sales last year. "You have an amazing collection," he continued before pulling one of them from the shelf.

"Thank you. Wanna play that?" I stood next to him and glanced at the music he picked.

He nodded and handed me the record. Giving me a shy smile before claiming a spot on the couch.

I joined Kai once the record started playing and tried to remember the last time I was this excited to share experiences with someone.

Bonnie Raitt's song was playing in the background. Kai's stare was intensified by the low light from the floor lamp reflecting off his eyes. He started humming the tune and slowly closed his eyes while he tilted his head, swaying left and right in sync with the music. The tip of his tongue darted out to moisten his lips. "I love this song," he said as he exhaled, his lips parting.

"Kai?" I whispered under my breath.

THIRTEEN: WYATT

Slowly, he opened his eyes. They sparkled when he gazed at me. "Yeah?"

I swallowed hard before continuing. "Can I kiss you?"

He stood up and I couldn't take my eyes off of him. I followed his every move. He reached out a hand, "Dance with me first?"

I let him pull me up. I didn't know how to dance, and I couldn't remember the last time I had. But to get a chance to finally kiss him, I'd figure out how to waltz.

I'd do anything.

He grabbed my other hand and he wrapped both of them around his waist, resting them above the curve of his ass. When his arms wrapped around my neck, our faces were inches apart. He started swaying his hips and I attempted to follow his lead.

The chorus of the song began. The warmth of his breath was hotter than the summer sun. The way his hands played with my hair was intoxicating. I closed my eyes to enjoy every sensation.

"Do you like that?" he asked, our bodies swaying as one.

All I managed to do was nod. I opened my eyes and found him staring at my lips. This man was driving me crazy and he had no idea. I didn't know what I wanted more, his body flushed with mine, his hands caressing my hair or his lips on mine.

My heart was beating so hard, my body was vibrating with each pulse. I moved my hand to his front, tracing his abs through his tight t-shirt, slowly moving up his chest then around his neck. I lowered my head and moved his closer to mine. Feeling our breaths mingled between us, I ghosted his soft lips. All my nerve endings gathered around my mouth. I pulled away just a little and then we kissed again, harder this time. He opened to give me access to his sweet mouth and my tongue dived in. We continued our dance, only this time it was our lips. We kissed with abandon, willing time to stop and for the music to never end.

The doorbell rang and broke the spell we were under. The awkwardness that I could've sworn would follow never arrived. Instead, Kai stole another kiss before he answered the door. *Damn you, pizza delivery guy!*

"Oh, hi! Is Wyatt home?" Avery's voice woke me out of my stupor.

"Yeah, Wyatt's here. I'm Kai by the way."

Avery peeked through the opened door, confusion all over his face. "I just came by to say hey, I didn't know you had company," he said with an awkward wave.

"I have a large Hawaiian Pizza for Wyatt," the pizza delivery guy called out, joining the commotion.

"Oh, for Christ's sake," I grumbled.

"Yeah, I'll take it," Kai said, pulling his wallet out of his pocket to pay.

I took the opportunity to grab Avery's attention and mouthed *Please go*, hoping Kai wouldn't see my attempt to kick my cockblocker of a friend out of my house. "We just got back from the beach and we're really tired," I said when he didn't move.

Avery looked between me and Kai putting two and two together causing his eyes to dance with mischief. "Well, nice to meet you, Kai." he offered a hand.

Kai better not invite him in for pizza.

"Thanks for checking in," I said, urging Avery to fuck off with my eyes. "I'll see you later. At. Work," I stressed, wondering if my gritted smile was enough to get the point across.

Avery laughed because the asshole was enjoying this. "Oh,

THIRTEEN: WYATT

yeah, sure. I hope to see you around, Kai."

"That would be cool. Nice to meet you too, Avery," Kai said before closing the door. "Well, that was fun. Now, where were we?"

Fourteen: Wyatt

Neat Freak

After closing the door and placing the box of pizza on the counter, Kai sauntered back to me and kissed me back to oblivion. All thoughts of Avery's impromptu visit and the delivery guy were forgotten. That kiss was the best I'd ever had. I wanted more of him. I lifted my hands to cup his face, but a sharp pain traveled down my shoulder blade and made me wince.

"Are you okay?" he asked, pulling away to study my face.

"Yeah, just a little sore is all."

"Can I do something?" he asked.

"Nah, I'll be fine."

He studied me for a while. "Would a massage help?"

"Maybe… I think so." I stepped back and attempted to stretch my shoulder. I knew I was older, but I wasn't out of shape. Those waves did a number on my body and every crash had been worth every sparkle in Kai's gorgeous honey eyes.

He looked at me through his lashes with a small smile on his soft lips. "Can I do it?" he asked before his tongue darted out, my eyes following the movement.

I couldn't speak. The thought of his hands all over me sent

FOURTEEN: WYATT

shockwaves down my spine.

"Don't worry, I know how. My cousin Mikaela and I gave each other massages whenever we were sore from being tossed around by massive waves while surfing."

"If you're sure."

"Do you have any lotion or oil?"

I know he meant for the massage, but my mind went somewhere else *again*, causing certain parts of me to throb. A reminder that it had been a long while since I enjoyed the company of another man. "Do you prefer one over the other?" I asked, my voice raspier than normal. I cleared my throat.

"Oh, whatever you like?" he responded, his eyes traveling up and down my body made my mouth dry.

I went to the bedroom, momentarily forgetting what I was there for because I was still thinking about his lips. I hurried to the bathroom and went through the cabinet under the sink looking for something Kai could use for the massage. I finally settled on an old bottle of body oil I didn't even know I had. I felt a little lightheaded, unsure if it was from standing up too quickly or because every ounce of my blood had gathered in my now painfully erect cock. *This ought to be interesting.*

Kai was sitting on the couch, waiting for me. "Should we do it on the couch or your bed?"

He was fucking killing me and he had no idea.

I strategically placed the bath towel I'd grabbed on my way out, in front of me to hide my erection. "We can do it in the bedroom."

"That's probably better. I don't think your couch can fit both of us."

I led the way to my bedroom, while he followed. I glanced over to look at him and found him staring at my ass, but he averted his gaze when he realized that I had glanced over my shoulder.

Kai said something but I didn't understand what it was because all I could hear was the drumming of my pulse gushing blood through my head. "What's that?" I asked.

"I said, this is a big place for one person," he repeated.

I just shrugged. "Elijah spends the night sometimes." We had reached my bedroom and my brain had stalled.

"I need to wash my hands."

"Over there," I managed to even point to the bathroom door with the bottle of oil in my hand.

I was standing by the foot of the bed still covering myself with the towel when he returned from the bathroom. Unsure of what I was supposed to do, I offered him a nervous smile. It wasn't like I'd never had a massage before, but somehow this felt different.

"Why don't you go ahead and take your clothes off and lay on the bed?" he suggested, looking between me and the bed.

I stared at him. "All of them?" I asked.

"Where do you hurt?"

Needing water, I cleared my throat. "My back, my arms, my legs."

"So everywhere? I'm gonna have to charge you more," he teased, trying to ease the tension that I could've sliced with a dull knife. "Take everything off, but your underwear, then lay that towel on your bed so we don't make a mess."

I moaned inwardly when I turned my back to Kai and reluctantly dropped the towel on my bed. I pulled off my shirt and folded it before placing it next to the towel.

"You're so adorable," he chuckled, "military habit?"

"No, I just prefer everything tidy."

FOURTEEN: WYATT

"Ok, neat freak."

I turned so I could roll my eyes at him and continued undressing. I undid my belt, unzipped my pants, and pulled them off. I was about to fold them just like my shirt, but to prove that I wasn't a neat freak, I tossed them unceremoniously to the floor. "See, that doesn't bother me one bit," I insisted. *What was up with this man who made me do things I wouldn't usually do?* I was expecting another round of teasing, but Kai was quiet for once. He pointed to the bed and I laid on my stomach.

The pop of the bottle's cap opening broke the silence in the room. All I could hear was the sound of our heavy breathing and the ticking hand of the clock. Moments later, Kai's warm hands landed on my shoulders, applying pressure as he moved his fingers toward the center of my back up to the base of my neck and back. His thumbs dug deep into the spot where my spine met my shoulder blades. He started softly and then increased the pressure.

He dragged his elbows down both sides of my back parallel to my spine and I couldn't help but groan.

"Relax, you're too tense. I'm not going to be able to help your muscles stretch out if you don't trust me and let go a bit," Kai said, willing me to relax with a quiet, but direct order.

Easy for you to say. I was already feeling my erection jamming into the towel. I hadn't been with a man this intimately since my ex in the Marines. It worked out for me, considering I hadn't wanted to be close to anyone.

"That's it, Wyatt, let go. Feel my touch and let the warmth release your tight and sore muscles."

Kai dug into my neck, squeezing and sliding his strong hands down both sides. He ended the firm caress with a tight squeeze of my shoulders where he paused with his firm hands before easing back up my neck.

He straddled my lower back and sat down on my nearly naked butt. I hoped my briefs could contain my impatient cock. When he leaned forward to massage from my shoulders to my neck, he naturally lifted off of me and then slowly sat back down again as his hands traveled down my back. His moving around and rubbing his boardshorts-clad ass against mine was intoxicating. It hadn't gotten by me that he had a perfectly round ass. I'd seen it in his tight-fitting jeans and wetsuit. I was an ass man, and this man had one of the finest specimens I'd seen. When we danced earlier, I may have allowed my fingers to slide down a bit so I could feel the curve from his lower back to his round ass.

Every time he sat back and smashed my dick into the bed, I somehow got harder. If he kept it up, I was going to blow my load.

"Can you spread your legs apart for me?" he asked.

Can I spread my legs apart? What the... "Uh, yeah... for?" I asked nervously.

"I'm going to sit between them so I can access your upper and lower back easier. I'll try to move the tension down and away from your neck, is that okay with you?"

What the fuck happens when you get to my waist? I wondered, feeling another inch of girth swelling in my crotch.

"Yeah sure, it feels pretty good so far," I lied. Who the fuck was I kidding? It felt out of this world, and I needed release. I hesitated another moment before I widened the space between my legs. Not even two seconds later, his legs were touching my inner thighs and I wondered how much longer I'd be able to last.

FOURTEEN: WYATT

Kai popped the lid on the oil again and I waited for him to pour it over my back, "Is it cold?" he asked, drizzling it slowly over my exposed skin.

"It's perfect."

Had I said that out loud?

He shifted to his knees when he leaned forward, putting his weight onto my back. He started at the center of my spine and fanned out to my sides an inch at a time, his hands stroking their way down to my ass. His knee was pressed against my crack and was nudging my balls, driving me fucking insane.

"How's that Wyatt, feeling relaxed? I'm going to lean an elbow into your back muscles okay? Do not tighten up, just ride with the movement," he whispered.

I grunted something incoherent from the pleasure I was feeling when he leaned forward, his crotch pressing against my ass. *Wait? Was that his hard cock pressing against me?* There was no denying he was rock hard and felt him brushing himself against me as he tried to disguise the motion by digging into my back with an elbow. I was reeling from the pressure from both points of contact.

"You're doing a great job, Kai. I think I'm good now. You're amazing," I said.

"Shhhh, we're no way near done," he announced. "Lift off the bed for a second and let's pull these down okay?" He tapped my hips and moved his fingers under the waistband of my briefs.

I may have groaned. I wasn't sure because I lost my fucking mind when he pulled off my underwear, his warm hands keeping contact with my legs the entire time.

Kai moved my briefs down my legs, releasing them from each one. Staying near my feet, he brought both of his hands up the inside of my legs, crawling toward my inner thighs. His fingers walked as he massaged, moving inch by inch until he was caressing my upper thighs. My butt cheeks instinctively clenched shut when his hands brushed under my sack. The moment his hand touched my balls, my erection throbbed and jolted alive again.

I heard the lid pop again and felt him drizzling oil over my ass cheeks. I could feel a bit of it creeping into my ass crack and down toward my balls.

Kai brought his hands to my ass cheeks and clenched each one in a separate hand, digging his fingers into them as he rubbed hard.

"It's getting hot in here," he said.

"You can take off your shirt if you want. Go ahead and turn on the ceiling fan. It's getting warm for me too."

I turned my head to the side, watching him stand up from the bed. He had his back to me as he peeled off his University of Hawai'i t-shirt and made his way to the switch. His beautiful mocha skin was smooth and with the exception of his scar that ran from his elbow to his forearm, his skin was perfect as it laid over a broad back, large for a guy his size. His V-shaped back muscles disappeared into a small lean waist. He was a vision and I swallowed hard at the sight. My eyes traveled down to the backs of his calves, just below his bold printed shorts. They were lean but muscular and perfectly smooth like his entire body. I hungered to see what I expected to be his round ass which was hidden inside his ever-present board shorts.

Kai turned around after flicking the fan switch on and caught my stare. He smiled and his eyes sparkled, reflecting light in an otherwise dim room. He made no attempt to hide his gaze

FOURTEEN: WYATT

as it moved over my naked body.

"You look amazing," he whispered, no shyness or fear, just a statement of fact as he continued staring.

"Thank you," I answered, before flipping over and exposing my painful erection.

"Can I take off my shorts? I'd like to be comfortable too," Kai asked, never breaking eye contact.

He had his fingers on the string that held his baggy shorts up. I could see his obliques exposed as he tugged his fingers down, pushing the shorts down to an obscene level. *Fuck, he's beautiful.*

All I could do besides craning my neck so I could take in his incredible body was nod my head in agreement.

I watched him untie the string, and separate the Velcro with a tearing sound before his shorts were open. He eyed me and then looked down to his waist as he let the shorts drop to the floor. His swollen dick popped out with a bounce after they slid down, revealing a gorgeous smooth piece of meat. It was thick, circumcised, and had smooth nuts hanging below. I knew I wanted it in my mouth.

I sat up, placing my feet over the side of the bed. "Come here," I ordered, spreading my legs apart to make space for him to kneel between them. "I need you, Kai," I moaned.

He walked across the room. Finally seeing him naked for the first time proved I'd been correct, this man was a vision of lean tightness. He had the perfect amount of muscle that was defined, but not overly so.

Kai stood in front of me, looking from my eyes to my throbbing dick.

I glanced at my erection, giving him all the permission to do anything to my body.

He kneeled in front of me, between my knees before pulling my cock toward his mouth. He lifted his head so our eyes met, grinning.

I watched his lips slide over my dick, taking its entire nine-inch length into his mouth in one swift movement. I gasped, my whole body was trembling. He held me in his throat so I flexed, swelling in his warmth. I was embarrassed by the tremor coursing through my thighs and yet not caring because the pleasure was blinding.

"Fuck, that's good." I grabbed the sides of his head, guiding my cock in and out of his sweet mouth.

He grabbed my balls and squeezed them, massaging them in his free hand as he slid the other up and down my shaft which passed his wet lips. Gently touching my stomach, he pushed me back onto the bed, coming higher to his knees, and dropped his face onto my cock again. He moved up and down like an expert, tonguing my head and kneading my balls.

"You're hard as fuck, Wyatt. You like your dick in my mouth?" he asked. He was still holding my cock and his inquiring face was glossed with lust and desire that could rival mine.

"What do you think?" I reached around the back of his head and guided him back onto my cock.

"Mmmff," was all I heard as the back of his head bobbed up and down, slurping on my shaft.

I sat back up and watched him expertly swallowing every inch of me. He had a real talent, and I was enjoying Kai's silky hot mouth. The velvet of his tongue was driving me insane. I grabbed his head and pulled him off my cock. "Stand up, Kai," I demanded, gripping his hands tightly as he lifted himself from his knees. I moved my hands around to his ass, cupping a perfectly sculpted ass cheek in each hand. His cock was inches

FOURTEEN: WYATT

from my face while I played with his ass, moving my fingers along his crack, and pinching each round cheek.

"I'm going to have to admit something to you," I began.

"Let me guess, you're an ass man," he said, no hint of scorn, just an obvious guess based on my manhandling of it. "Good thing. I'm very lucky then," he added, shoving his cock against my face.

That was all I needed to hear from him. I took his cock in my mouth, pulling him forward, pumping my mouth full of him. I deep throated his thick seven-inch cock and he tasted so fucking good. I love my men smooth, and he checked every box when it came to my fantasies. I was in heaven as he fed his dick into my mouth, controlling my head while he face-fucked me. I moved my hands lower and stuck them between his ass cheeks. I felt around with a finger, looking for the honey hole until I swept the tip of a finger over it. His dick pulsed and swelled as soon as he felt pressure against his tight little pucker.

I moaned with a mouthful of cock at the desire that surged through me after discovering my target.

I pulled off with a pop. "Amazing ass Kai, it's perfect," I admitted, going crazy with the obsessive craving. I needed to have this ass, yet I was afraid to admit how much I wanted him, afraid of it being so good that I'd lose control.

"It's yours if you want it," he moaned, writhing under my touch and moving his asshole down onto my finger.

"Turn around."

Kai pulled out of my mouth with his honey eyes looking down at me, gauging my desire, seeing if I were really up to what he offered. I grabbed his hips and turned him around, showing him I was all in.

He now stood in front of me while I still sat on the edge of the bed admiring his back and how it led down to the round fullness of two smooth globes. I kissed his lower back and he tensed with a slight shiver from the anticipation. I moved my tongue across his ass, using my fingers to part his cheeks slightly before nibbling at them. He reached around his back and pushed my face into his ass, begging me to explore more territory. So I parted his cheeks and moved my tongue from the small of his back down to his hole. I flickered my tongue over his tight entrance and then gripped his hips, moving him back harder into my waiting mouth.

"Oh yeah…. fuck that's hot," he whispered, holding my hands that were firmly planted on his hips. "Please don't stop," he shivered, his knees trembling.

"That's good, Kai, beg for more," I growled, moving my mouth over his sweet ass cheeks, probing my tongue, and biting his skin gently.

"Get inside me, I need to feel you inside me."

I reached for the drawer of my nightstand and pulled it open, finding an unopened box of rubbers. I tore the box quickly and pulled out a strip of foiled condoms. I couldn't get one open quick enough as I stared at the most fucking exquisite ass I'd ever seen. I wanted, no, I needed to be inside him, to feel him wrapped around me. This could be a bad move. My cock was saying *you need to be inside him now,* but my heart was saying *tread carefully Wyatt, you could fall for this one.*

I slid the rubber over my swollen shaft, still holding Kai with my other hand as he faced away from me. I grabbed the oil since I hadn't thought I'd need lube anytime soon. I drizzled some on my fingers and slid them between his cheeks, once again seeking that sweet spot I so craved with every fiber in

FOURTEEN: WYATT

my body.

I pressed against his entrance, waiting for him to give up the barrier and welcome me in.

"Easy, it's been a while."

"You're sure you're ready for this?" I asked, wondering if my girth would fit in his small tight hole.

"Trust me, I'm more than ready."

I pulled him backward and pushed his back so he'd lean forward, exposing his ass to my rod. I held his hips with one hand and my cock with the other, guiding my throbbing piece toward the promised land. My dick's head met his hole and I gently flicked it over his hole, transferring more lube over it.

"Sit back Kai, you take control."

He reached back and supported himself on my knees and lowered himself onto my shaft, moving tenderly as his hole took a measure of its invader. He let the head slip in and paused, moaning heavily as he threw his head back. "Fuck... you're huge, but I want you in me. I want to feel all of you."

He slowly absorbed my ever-growing cock inside his hungry ass until he was sitting on my lap. I leaned forward to reach around and felt his throbbing cock waiting to be gripped tightly as I gyrated my hips underneath him, slowly digging deeper into him. Kai leaned back into me, and I supported all of him as he straddled my lap, his legs dangling in the air as I bobbed up and down. He put his hands above his head, grabbing my hair as he rested in the groove of my neck so I buried my nose in his soft hair. I pulled Kai down my shaft and groaned when he took all of me. Wanting to savor being buried in his sweetness, I explored his defined abs and chest. "How you doin', Kai?" I asked before I stroked up his cock causing a bead of pre-cum to glisten on his engorged head.

He ground his ass against me and I couldn't stop my moan. "Better than I imagined. I want to see your face when you cum."

"Stand up," I ordered, gripping his hips, and lifting him off my dick.

I spun him around and pulled him into my arms, my mouth planting hard on his. He put his arms around my neck, offering himself to me fully. Our sweaty bodies rubbing against each other with both our cocks begging for relief.

I dropped to my knees and took his swollen dick into my mouth, tasting his cum as I slid my mouth over him, taking him deep into my throat. He held my head and forced his hips up, fucking my mouth with urgency while I stroked myself. I could tell from his flexing dick that he was close, so I moved my mouth off of him.

"You want to shoot in my mouth or—"

"I want you back inside me," he growled, eyeing my dick that I held in my hands. "I want more of that," he nodded his head toward my raging erection.

I stood back up and grabbed him from the back of his knees and yanked him to the edge of the bed, his feet on my chest, exposing himself to me. I grabbed my cock and slapped it against his hole a couple of times.

"This what you want?" I asked, holding my hard-on which was getting harder as I stared at his tight body laying back, welcoming me.

"Yes, Wyatt, all of you." He had his cock in his hand, jacking it hard.

I pressed the fat head of my dick against his hole and slammed it in hard, staying there until he opened his eyes that had just rolled into the back of his head. He smiled up at

FOURTEEN: WYATT

me. "Just like that," he groaned, fisting his thick meat hard.

I plowed into him hard, pounding harder when he moaned with his head rolling back and forth, lost in pleasure. Staring at his sweat-glistened body lying on my bed, drove me mad. Grabbing his ankles, I lifted his ass and plunged into him again.

"Fuck, Wyatt… that's it, harder."

Kai was panting and writhing on the bed as I controlled his legs. I was keeping them in my charge as I gave him what he was begging for. He wanted it hard and deep, well, then he was going to get exactly what he wanted. I had a huge need to please him and fulfill his needs. I wanted to be the man he desired.

"I'm fucking close," I said, grunting louder as I pounded on his hole.

He grabbed my hips, yanking me into him harder, gritting his teeth in pleasure. "Give it to me!" he yelled, staring directly into my eyes, begging me to keep it up.

Kai's moaning fueled my fire to keep going.

I moved his hand away from his cock and gripped it tight, stroking up and down and keeping rhythm with my cock plunging into his hungry asshole.

"Fuck Kai, you're amazing, so hot. I fucking love your ass," I growled, gritting my teeth, my jaw clamped shut when I felt my load churning.

I kept stroking his cock when he threw his arms over his head, completely exposing himself to me and giving over all control. "I'm so close," he yelled, looking at me.

"It's coming baby, I'm almost there," I growled, knowing I was close too, and my load was about to blast free. "Here it comes… fuuucckkk."

"Give it to me, yeah," he moaned, reaching his hands to wrap around my neck when I leaned forward, pumping every last drop of my release.

I climaxed just in time to see Kai's cock give up its prize as his load jetted across his chest. I collapsed onto him, and he wrapped his arms and legs around me.

"That was so good Wyatt. So good."

I turned my face to his and our mouths connected.

Fifteen: Wyatt

Don't Be Weird

Elizabeth and Avery were in the middle of a serious conversation about remodeling when I entered the office.

"The contractor is ready in a couple of weeks? But we don't have a plan drawn yet," Elizabeth said, her eyes closed in exacerbation.

"I know babe, but we'll have to wait until next year if we don't take this. Every single contractor on the island is booked and they just happened to have a last-minute cancellation," Avery explained.

They both turned when the door closed behind me. Avery's eyes lit up and he nodded in my direction before a smirk cracked across his face. "So, how was the pizza?" he asked before crossing his arms.

I rolled my eyes but couldn't keep the smile off my face. "Delicious."

Elizabeth watched me approach my desk.

"What?" I asked, hating their scrutiny.

Elizabeth glanced at Avery and he just gave her his shit-eating grin. "What's with the smile? What's this I hear about pizza?" she asked, crossing her arms and sitting on top of her desk with a smirk.

Avery leaned on the same desk, studying me with a knowing look. "You look goofy as shit," he teased, earning him an elbow from Elizabeth to his ribs. "What? He does," he chuckled, unable to stifle his laugh.

I shook my head, a little embarrassed. "Fuck off!" I flipped him off and walked past them to get a cup of coffee. Thankful that my back was turned to hide the redness creeping up my face, I added sugar and creamer to my cup.

"Leave Wyatt alone," Elizabeth said while they followed me. "I like it when you smile," she continued, standing next to me while fixing herself a fresh cup of coffee.

"Aren't you one bit curious?" Avery taunted me when he stood behind us. "Because I am."

I was sandwiched between my two best friends, unable to hide my silly grin with the hilarity of this situation.

"Dude, you're grinning like a maniac!" he continued and wrapped his arms around my shoulder when I tried to head back to my desk. "So should I guess that last night went well? With the delicious pizza and all?"

"Avery," Elizabeth slapped his arm, playfully.

"Is there a problem with the remodel?" I said, trying to change the subject to anything, but me.

They'd been on a mission to find a contractor and an architect to draw up the plans since we'd finally agreed to remodel. Because I trusted them with that kind of stuff, I stayed clear of the project, figuring that one less captain on this remodeling ship, the better.

"So, you're not gonna tell us more about last night?" Avery asked after I peeled his arm off me.

FIFTEEN: WYATT

"Leave him alone, he'll tell us when and if he's ready," Elizabeth was as tactful as ever.

"Thanks, E, but there's nothing to tell." I didn't want to discuss last night when I was still wrapping my head around the situation. "So, what's the problem with the remodel?"

"Oh, Avery finally found a contractor, but their only opening is in two weeks," she explained.

"That's good, right? We can get started sooner than planned," I said.

"It would be, only if we had someone to draw up the plans before then. I don't know if we can find an architect to draft anything with this short of a notice," Avery explained, dramatically banging his hand on his desk.

"I might know someone," I blurted before I could change my mind. I immediately thought of Kai and hoped he could help us. I knew he just graduated, but how hard could it be? Our office was small and we weren't planning to build anything elaborate. It was just to update the space with more windows and a waiting area. Plus, I could use an excuse to see him again. I fished my phone out of my pocket and started texting him. *Remember when I told you that we're renovating our office? Looks like we have a contractor, but no architect. Would you consider doing it?* I looked up after pressing send and two sets of eyes were on me, again.

"You do?" Elizabeth raised her eyebrow.

"Yes, I met a guy recently, and he's a new architect and doing freelance work."

"So, this *guy*, would he happen to like pizza?" Avery asked, using his interrogation tactics on me. He walked around my desk to take a peek at my screen.

"Dude, do you mind?" I pulled my cell closer to my chest

and pushed him away. That had been the wrong move since it only fueled his ribbing.

Elizabeth's phone started ringing and I was thankful for the interruption. To my dismay, she ignored the call and followed Avery's line of questioning, "Okay, now I'm curious to know who this guy is, you *never* act this weird about *some* guy."

"What happened to he'll tell us when he's ready?" I asked and pushed Avery again while he attempted to grab my phone. "Dude, go away. You're acting like a teenager."

"Oh, I'm *the teenager*? You're the one who had a hot date and won't tell us about him," Avery said pointing at my face.

"So, wait, is Mr. Pizza and Mr. Architect the same guy?" Elizabeth pushed.

My phone dinged before I had a chance to answer her question. Two text messages from Kai came in, and I read them close to my face to avoid Avery's prying eyes. The idiot was now standing behind me. The first one said, *'Anything for you'* which he followed with a smile heart emoji. The other message was *'Want me to come by your office?'*

After texting *'Yes, please.'* I turned my attention to both of them and gave them a stern warning. "His name is Kai and he's on his way to check out this dump. Don't be weird, please."

Fifteen minutes later, Kai arrived on his bicycle. Through the large glass window, he pointed at a space close to the entrance, silently asking if it was okay to park it there.

I gave him a thumbs up and got up to meet him at the door. I didn't miss the smirk on my friends' faces when I passed by their desks. "Don't make me regret inviting him here," I warned them once again, unable to hide the smile creeping

FIFTEEN: WYATT

across my face when I looked at Kai.

"Kai, you might remember my friend Avery. This is his wife and his much better half, Elizabeth." I introduced everyone before we could get inside. They'd been waiting by the door after I stepped outside, and I hoped they didn't make fools of themselves.

"Nice to meet you," Kai extended his hand and greeted Elizabeth first. "Good to see you again," he offered his hand to Avery next.

We all walked inside, conscious of the state of our office. We always kept it clean, but the place was showing its age. The walls had dents from moving gear around, and the wooden floor was covered with scratches. Even the wide windows with a scenic view of the water and the dock had begun to lose their battle to the salty sea air.

"Nice to meet you too, Kai. And thank you for being here, you're a lifesaver," Elizabeth said.

"Don't thank me yet," Kai winked, giving her and Avery a warm smile.

"What do you think about this dump?" Avery asked.

I was glad Avery was behaving and not mentioning pizza or anything else to embarrass Kai.

Kai looked around the office, and I held my breath waiting for his opinion. It shouldn't matter to me what he thought, but just like my house, I wanted him to like this part of my life too. "This place is charming," he finally said. "And that view, I could stay here all day."

Then do.

I blew out a breath, relieved that he didn't hate the place. "So, can you do it?"

"Of course, easy, no problem," Kai said. "I can draft the plans in a couple of days."

Elizabeth, who was excitable as always, leaped toward Kai and hugged him. "Thank you, thank you," she gushed.

"So, Kai, how do you know Wyatt?" Avery asked, the mischief returning to his fucking face.

Kai's face turned red and the need to save him from embarrassment kicked in. "Leave him alone. He's here to save our asses, remember?" I stressed before Kai had a chance to answer. I'd tell my friends how we met later when Kai wasn't around.

"What? I was just asking?" Avery chuckled. "He trusted you enough to share a pizza, so…"

"Whatever. I'm gonna show Kai around," I said, hell-bent on keeping Avery in check. I figured it was safer to give Kai a tour of the office. Starting from the outside.

"Your friends seem nice," Kai said when we were finally outside. He turned and waved to my nosy friends who were watching us through the glass windows. They even sipped from their cups of coffee while observing our every move.

"They're nosy as fuck, but they mean well," I said and gave Avery the bird when he started waving back at us animatedly. "They're my only family," I added in a whisper.

"I'm happy to have met them then."

I showed Kai our fleet to get some alone time away from Avery and Elizabeth's prying eyes. We were hanging out in one of the catamarans and enjoying the beautiful summer day. "What's on your mind?" I asked Kai who was looking at the horizon, lost in his thoughts. I grabbed his hand and brushed it against my lips.

He turned to face me and hesitated for a bit before answering. "You said something about your father a few days ago and I

FIFTEEN: WYATT

still couldn't believe it, you know?"

"It was a long time ago," I shrugged.

"When was the last time you saw him?"

"When he kicked me out. He moved to Oregon after that." The bitterness that I felt whenever I thought about my father tried to sour the mood, but I wouldn't let that ruin my day with Kai.

Thankful that he stopped pressing, I asked, "Wanna go for a spin?"

His excitement pushed aside any thoughts of my father. He always had the ability to brighten my day. "Take me, Captain," he saluted.

Sixteen: Kai

Breakfast Carrot Muffins

D*ing! Ding!* The sound of the metal antique bell ringing paired with the delicious scents of fresh-baked sweets and coffee had become an integral part of my walks to the pier every morning since I'd arrived in Friday Harbor. Only this time, Wyatt had joined me. *Had it only been a couple of weeks?* The time had been dragging me along with my guilt, but after meeting Wyatt, my life was finally turning around.

"Hi Kai," Andrea called from behind the register while waving at us.

"Mahalo! Or is it Aloha?" Pete, the barista and Andrea's boyfriend, asked.

"Aloha, Pete. Mahalo means *thank you*, so technically, both are fine. A little out of sequence, but fine."

"Just how often are you here?" Wyatt asked while we walked to get in line. "Everyone knows you here. I don't even think Pete knows my name, if he does, he's never used it."

"I'm here every day, I love it here." I looked back at him while taking another step to the counter once the line went down to two people in front of us.

SIXTEEN: KAI

"We'll have two of those carrot muffins and two mochas," Wyatt blurted without saying hello. The same person who complained about not being called by his name.

"Wait, did you say carrot muffin?" I chuckled.

"Sure did."

"Those are muffins?" I asked as I pointed to the glass countertop showcasing the items in question.

"Yes," he deadpanned.

"They're covered with frosting." I glanced at the counter and found Andrea trying to hide a smile.

"That's not frosting, it's a topping, see the granola bits on top?" Wyatt explained as if it was the most mundane thing on the planet.

"I think those are carrot cakes with cream cheese frosting."

"No, they're *breakfast* carrot muffins with toppings. Look at their shapes, Kai."

I was amazed that he was saying all of this with a straight face. "I'm looking at them. They're shaped like cupcakes, *Wyatt*."

Andrea turned her back on us and Pete was now watching what I could only assume was the craziest interaction he'd ever witnessed. All of it was so comical, but I couldn't seem to stop.

"Oh, Kai, you're precious," Pete said, in between plating our *muffins* and handing them to us over the counter. "I'll bring your coffee to your table."

"We'll be outside. Thanks, Pete," Wyatt said.

The look of surprise Pete gave Wyatt after he'd used his name was priceless. I hoped that the surveillance cameras inside the café captured that moment. That couldn't be the first time Wyatt ever acknowledged Pete, could it?

I winked at them both after I settled our order.

Andrea pointed at Wyatt and gave me a thumbs up while

mouthing the words, *is he okay?*

"He's fine," I whispered while covering the side of my mouth closest to Wyatt. The not-so-subtle move earned both Andrea and me a glare which was followed by a headshake that ultimately led to him walking out the door to get one of the spots outside.

"I hope we didn't make him upset," Pete said, putting his arm around Andrea's shoulder once Wyatt was out of earshot.

"Nah, he'll be fine. It's good for him, but I better go do damage control."

The metal chair was cold when I joined Wyatt at the table closest to the sidewalk overlooking the water. He slouched in one of the chairs, one arm was resting on a neighboring chair, while the other was resting on the table. He looked like a freaking model, striking a pose.

"Well, that was fun!" I teased, grabbing the white saucer with the gold trim containing the muffin and examining it.

"For what it's worth, I think you're right. Those are cupcakes. But on the random chances, I'm lucky enough to come here with Elijah, he calls them muffins. And since he's learning how to read, Andrea changed the menu for him. So they're cupcake-shaped muffins," he explained before taking a big bite, leaving a smear of frosting on his upper lip.

"That's cute," I smiled, wondering if I'd ever meet Elijah. "You have something..." I pointed to his lips.

Wyatt darted his tongue out and licked the soft frosting, taking me back to when I was the one getting licked. I wished I could've licked it for him, but it wasn't good table manners out in public.

"Here's your coffee gentleman." Pete placed a hand on my shoulder before continuing, "Can I get you anything else?"

SIXTEEN: KAI

Wyatt's eyes focused on the hand resting on my shoulder before his grey eyes flicked back to Pete's face. "We're good, thanks."

"What made you decide to move to San Juan?" He took a sip of his coffee after Pete left, his eyes never leaving mine. I'd since learned that the brightness of his grey eyes mirrored his mood. The stormy grey hue I saw the night we met had been non-existent ever since. "Most people would have chosen Seattle, you know, the bigger city," he continued before he enjoyed another sip of his mocha.

His question, although a very simple one, was loaded with so many nuances I wasn't sure I wanted to discuss anything right then and there, especially not before coffee. But I couldn't expect him to continue opening up if I wasn't willing to do the same.

"Forget I asked," Wyatt said, watching me play with my fork and the muffin.

I became hyper-aware of my fumbling when under his piercing scrutiny. Exhaling a breath, I tried to calm my hands. "San Juan Islands just seemed like a nice place. I'm surprised you didn't order a black coffee?"

"Actually, I hate black coffee. I like my coffee sweet," he confessed.

My mouth dropped open at the revelation. "I ordered you the wrong drink and you didn't say anything?" This man was the sweetest person on the planet, and he had no clue.

Instead of answering my question, Wyatt just smiled and took another sip.

We started our trek to The Cascade Mountain Range after our breakfast at the café. Wyatt was going to take me on an official date, but he wouldn't tell me where we were headed. I didn't care, as long as I was with him. We had an amazing time on our last road trip to the ocean and this date shouldn't be any different.

I rolled my window down when we entered a mountainous part of the freeway and I stuck a hand out. I loved the feeling of the cool breeze against my palm and made airplane motions with my hand. "Where are you taking me? You're not a serial killer, right? I really should've asked, before I got in," I teased.

"So impatient," Wyatt chuckled. "And no I'm not a serial killer. It's just I've always wanted to try my away game, you know?" Wyatt said while grinning ear to ear.

"Away game? That implies having a home game—or game in general. I don't think you have either."

"Hey, I got game. You're sitting there, right? That's because of my game," he quipped. He grabbed my hand to kiss it before putting it on his lap.

"We'll see," was all I could say. I focused my attention back on the hillsides covered with beautiful trees.

Seventeen: Wyatt

Do you trust me?

I wanted to impress him. That was the main reason why I'd decided to do this activity. I survived a rigorous Marine's boot camp, completed physical and mental training to be part of the Marine Corp Special Operatives, did two tours in Afghanistan, and jumped out of many airplanes, but I'd never once felt more anxious than what I felt trying to plan something for a date. This must be what they meant when they said butterflies in your stomach. Only it felt like a whole zoo decided to take residence in my gut. Even my hands trembled from the excitement.

"It's cool that you were in the Marines," Kai said, taking me out of my musing.

I shrugged it off as if it wasn't a big deal.

"Marines are hot. They're like nine out of ten on the scale," he continued.

Confused, I gave him a quick glance to gauge his level of seriousness, but his attention was outside admiring the stands of evergreen pine trees blanketing the hillside of the Cascade Mountain Range. "What scale?" I asked, and Kai finally glanced at me.

"You know the steam-o-meter scale for hotness." Kai looked at me as if I had two heads, and that ridiculous statement was the most common fact known to man. "Nine is the Marine, eight is the Navy, seven is the Airforce... you know," he explained.

"No, I don't know. That's literally the stupidest thing I've ever heard." I exchanged glances between the road and Kai who had his mouth open while shaking his head.

"So, you don't think Marines should be nine?"

"Kai, that's not the point. My point is that's not a real thing. You just made that up to pull my leg."

"Pull your leg? How old are you, gramps? Ninety?" he joked. "Wyatt, it's a real thing."

"No, it isn't."

"Wait a second, were you upset because you only ranked nine?"

"Don't be ridiculous," I replied. Although, if I was being completely honest, I hated that I only ranked nine to Kai, even with this stupid rating of his. With him, I wanted to be the best, but I knew that was childish. "I can't believe I'm about to ask this, but what gets a ten on your silly, *made-up* scale?"

Kai's smile widened and his face lit up. "Oh, look who's all curious now," he teased.

"So, who gets a ten?" I asked, embarrassed that I cared.

"Well, it could be the Navy, Airforce, or the Marines, but..." he hung on to the last statement. "They have to have a high rank. Men in uniform are very sexy and those with authority... even hotter. That's why they claim the top spots."

I took the next exit to our destination and I saw Kai watching me from the corner of my eye. I found a place to park, but before we climbed out of the truck, I needed to make things *very* clear. "I was a Lance Corporal. I had guys reporting to me while we were in deployment." I didn't know what made me say that, but it was too late to take it back.

"Is that right? Well, Lance Corporal Wyatt Miller, you just moved up to the top spot," he said before closing the distance between us and kissing me on the cheek.

Call me petty, but I felt like the king of the world. I looked at my rear-view mirror and was shocked by the grin spreading across my face. I can't remember the last time I smiled so hard that it hurt. It wasn't even nine o'clock and I was eager to enjoy the rest of our date.

"And Lance Corporal, I was just messing with you. There's no list, but it was adorable that you couldn't stand not being the best."

Adorable? I didn't think anyone had ever described me like that. "You're awful. I'm going to get you," I promised.

"I hope so."

"It's so beautiful out here?" Kai said when he stopped to look at the view below. "Great choice! I love hiking too, another thing we have in common. Water?" He grabbed a bottle of water from his backpack.

"Don't get too excited. Although I love to hike, it's not the reason why we're here." I gulped down the water he handed me. "You think I'd pick something low-key after the surfing show you displayed last time?" I motioned to have him turn around to put our water back in his backpack. That was the truth, I wanted to impress him and let him know that I'm more than just the man he saw broken down. There's more to me than a tormented soldier, but I wanted Kai to be proud of me for something.

"Is everything okay?" he turned his head around after a few seconds of silence.

"Yeah!" I answered, after zipping his backpack up and nudged him to keep going.

This hike was not for the faint of heart. The steep elevation required stamina, and I was thankful that Kai and I were in great shape. The trail was narrowing, and the trees were becoming thicker the higher we trekked.

"I need my jacket," Kai said. "My Hawaiian ass can't handle the cooler mountain temperature," he explained.

"What? You have a flaw?" I teased.

"Being cold is not a flaw. I'll take you to Hawai'i in the middle of summer and let's see how your pale ass handles that."

"How would you know my ass was pale?" I asked, knowing full well how he knew.

"Because I massaged that sexy thing," he growled and smacked my butt. "Just trust me, I have flaws," he admitted. I didn't miss the dark cloud that covered his eyes after that last statement.

He pulled his green windbreaker jacket out of his backpack. "Do you need yours?" he asked.

"Nah, my white ass can handle the cold," I teased to lighten the tension. I wanted to push more, but it wasn't my place. I knew as well as anyone, how hard it was to share something very personal and fearing judgment.

"Alright, Lance Corporal, lead the way. I'm dying to find out what you have in store for me."

"You're not going to ask for another clue?"

"Nope, surprise me!"

"My kind of guy," I said.

SEVENTEEN: WYATT

"But Wyatt," he raised one eyebrow.

"Yeah?"

"Let's be clear, surprise me... but don't disappoint me," he winked. Thankful that the playful side of him was back.

"You've got to be kidding me," Kai explained when we reached the summit of Mt. Si. There was a clearing the size of a football field and because the trees had been cut back, the view stretched over the lake and the foothills below. The sky was peppered with colorful paragliders that looked like birds flying above the valley.

"What?" I asked innocently. "You said you liked extremes and you'd try anything once, well this is me. If there's one thing I know how to do, and do well, it's paragliding." I walked closer to his side and tapped his butt. "You'll be okay. Besides, I love coming here on a nice clear day. It reminds me of when my squad used to jump out of airplanes for training."

Kai looked around nervously at a couple of people who were preparing to launch. I started to feel guilty for not letting him know ahead of time. This was pretty intense, and I didn't know how much he could handle.

"We don't have to do it, we could just watch my friends."

"Miller!" someone yelled. "Bro, what's up?"

I turned to the voice and found my Marine buddy that had said he'd also be there that day. "Hey, Brad, what's up?" We bumped fists and he turned to Kai.

"This is Kai." I introduced them and Kai extended his hand for a handshake.

"I see you're not set up yet, you're both gliding right?" Brad asked, turning back to me.

I turned to Kai and tried to school my face and keep my voice even. "We gonna do this? It's not too late to change your mind," I asked.

"Bring it on," he said, surprising me with his enthusiasm.

Eighteen: Kai

I Won't Let Us Fall

Wyatt laid the straps and harnesses on the ground while performing an inventory of everything we needed for this jump with laser focus. After going through the steps with me one more time, I couldn't help but notice how nervous he looked. He was biting his thumbnail as he glanced at our gear for what seemed like the tenth time.

"Are you nervous?" I asked, and he jolted his head up to meet my eyes, uncertainty written all over them.

"No, I just want to make sure that we have everything we need. Safety first, you know," he answered.

I was about to say something when Brad finished laying the blue and yellow sail on the ground. Its width covered twenty feet of the patchy land on top of the hill. Heavy-duty cables ran from the sail down to sets of harnesses with metal locking carabiners on each end.

"It's so nice to finally see you back up here," Brad said, giving Wyatt a tap on his shoulder once he reached us.

"Me too. Life, you know? It always gets in the way," Wyatt said.

"You okay though?" Brad asked.

Wyatt nodded 'yes' and stole a glance at me to assure me everything was fine.

"That's good, bro. Just holla if you need anything. We're here for you."

I'd heard that Marines, and the military for that matter, supported each other. Watching Wyatt and Brad's interaction convinced me of that strong bond, and I momentarily forgot my fear of jumping. *I can't believe I'm about to jump off this cliff... on purpose... for fun.*

And as if they could read my mind, Wyatt and Brad glanced in my direction.

"Let's get you boys set up," Brad announced.

"It's okay, bud. I got it," Wyatt said and Brad gave him a thumbs up before heading back to chat with his other friends.

Wyatt grabbed the harness from the ground and lifted it for inspection once again. "Let's get you strapped," he said.

"Strapped? That's kinky," I teased.

He rolled his eyes and shook his head. "Kai, this is serious," he said, his voice firm even though there was a sparkle in his gaze.

"I'm just kidding. I get chatty when I'm nervous."

"I just don't want anything to happen to you."

His eyes held mine and an overwhelming emotion prevented me from saying anything. It wasn't what he said, but the way he said it, like he would really be devastated if I got hurt. My eyes stung and my heart pounded. I was afraid, but no longer about the jump. I was afraid of something completely different when his grey eyes were staring at me. I buried the feeling that was starting to percolate in the deepest part of me. I couldn't afford to entertain it. All I managed to do was nod.

Wyatt continued to strap me into my harness starting from

EIGHTEEN: KAI

my legs to my waist, then to my shoulders. He started pulling to make sure they were secured and once he was satisfied, he put on his own harness.

There were so many layers about this man. I was learning how each new layer was as beautifully complex as the last.

"Don't be afraid," Wyatt assured me as we walked toward the edge of the cliff for our take-off after we'd attached ourselves to his paraglider.

The thing was, jumping off the cliff with just a piece of fabric and ropes separating us from the ground was the least thing that I was afraid of.

No.

It was the idea that I would do anything for this man that scared me the most. I looked down and everyone looked like ants from where I was standing. It made me feel small. The expansive blue sky without a single cloud and the wind blowing on my face sobered me up just as Wyatt continued.

"I won't let us fall," he told me as he checked our connections one more time.

Something told me that I already had.

"Do you trust me?" Wyatt asked, his smile rivaling the sun beaming down on us.

"With all my life."

Wyatt grabbed both of my hands and wrapped them around his waist resting on his abs. "We're gonna be running until there's no more land. We'll drop for a little before the wind catches our sail," he continued.

"Got it."

"On three," he said.

I nodded.

"One, two, three."

I kept pace with Wyatt when we ran to the edge of the cliff dragging our sail. And just like he said, we dipped for a few seconds causing my stomach to drop, and I squealed with the rush of adrenaline. My arms were still wrapped around him while I buried my face in his back. He maneuvered our sail, angling it to catch the best drift and after a couple of attempts, we were lifted up and into the warm air streams.

It was exhilarating! Never once had I imagined I'd jump off a cliff with just a piece of cloth and dozens of strings separating me from the ground. Well, that's not it, I was wrapped around the most beautiful specimen of a man I'd ever met. *'Do you trust me.'* he'd asked earlier. Call me crazy, but I did. I'd only known Wyatt for a couple of weeks, but I did trust him. He was so damn excited and dare I say happy when I said *'I'm all in.'*

"Woooohoooooooo!!!!! I'm flying," I yelled, spreading both of my arms out.

Wyatt laughed at my excitement when he glanced over his shoulder at me. "We are flying!"

I was torn between leaving my arms out or wrapping them around him. In the end, I wrapped them around him, probably tighter than I should have.

He grabbed one of my hands and brought it to his lips. The soft caress of his skin made my whole body tingle.

I am so screwed!

Wyatt lowered his left hand and that made our sail go that direction. He pointed to the majestic Mount Rainier in front of us, which was covered with snow at its highest elevations even on summer days. Once again, the exquisite surroundings made me feel insignificant.

"Thank you, Wyatt," I squeezed him tighter and leaned

against his back once again. "This is so incredible, and probably the best thing anyone has ever done for me."

"Anything for you Kai."

Nineteen: Wyatt

All the Cuts

This was a bad idea and I knew it the moment I said yes to Kai before I dropped him off last night. Just like the past few times, my sensible brain was MIA when it came to him and I stupidly agreed to meet him here at the Harbor Theatre, one of the oldest buildings in town. When I had arrived almost thirty minutes ago to wait for Kai, there had already been a line of twenty-somethings clad in jeans and t-shirts with the band's logo.

If he hadn't looked at me the way he did, I would've said no. What did his intense gaze mean? No one had ever looked at me like that before. I'd debated all day long and came very close to texting him that I couldn't go with a shitty excuse as to why. But the excitement on his face when I said I would, kept playing over and over again in my mind. I just couldn't find it in me to disappoint him.

The neon lights flashing *Chasing Thunder* were illuminating the classic marble façade of the theatre and me. Yes, I was willing to be fucking neon for a certain someone. My eyes darted along the length of the line which was now wrapped around the building with young people bathed in neon too.

NINETEEN: WYATT

I unlocked my phone once more, warring with the desire to cancel. I needed him to show up because I was two painful seconds away from talking myself out of going to this live performance.

I caught a whiff of fresh cologne that had a hint of citrus and immediately relaxed. I knew that scent. Within two excruciating heartbeats, Kai was standing beside me wearing a tight gray t-shirt that was partially tucked into his tight faded blue jeans. His black belt matched his distressed boots that were almost identical to what I was wearing.

"We look like twins," he greeted me before giving me a peck on the cheek. It was such a sweet gesture that felt natural between us.

"Copycat, I wore it best though," I teased back.

"If you say so," he winked. "I got our tickets earlier so we don't have to wait in line. Ready?"

I nodded in lieu of an actual response and let Kai lead the way to the entrance.

"You look great by the way," he said over his shoulder.

I rolled my eyes at him and said, "You're just saying that because we're practically matching."

"I'll take that as a thank you."

"I didn't intend it to be." I pulled him to my side and kissed the top of his head and he wrapped an arm around my waist.

We were greeted by loud music once we entered the door separating the hall from the lobby. I took a deep breath to keep my anxiety at bay and focused on Kai's voice and his hand in mine. The seats that I thought would be there were gone. Instead, there was a dance floor with groups of people dancing with drinks in their hands near the bar, while some people were congregated near the stage. There was an elaborate drum set in the back, a keyboard on the left, and two kinds of guitars on the right. In the center was a microphone on a stand that had a raccoon tail hanging from it that had appeared on their last album cover.

"Is it hot in here?" I asked Kai while I fanned my face with the top of my shirt, pulling it in and out rapidly.

"Not yet, but it will be once more people get in. Excuse me." Kai kept saying while we made our way to the front, bumping into a few other concertgoers who didn't seem to care about being jostled.

"No worries, bro," someone said, raising his plastic cup filled with beer to us and splashing it obnoxiously on other partiers.

I released Kai's hand for a moment to wipe my sweaty hands on my pants and that caught his attention. "I'm just gonna use the bathroom," I yelled into his ear before turning to leave.

"You okay?" he asked, placing his hand on my shoulder.

My mouth was getting dry and instead of saying anything back, I gave him a thumbs up. I followed the exit sign, choosing to walk along the wall to ensure the least amount of physical contact with these people. Kai was right, the room was getting more crowded and rowdier as more bodies entered the venue. I glanced back to where Kai was standing and found him watching me. I gave him another thumbs up and attempted a smile to ease the worry that was building on his face.

The bright and quiet bathroom was the reprieve I needed to calm down. I turned on the faucet and splashed cold water on my face. I looked at my reflection, "You can do this." After one more splash of cold water and another pep talk, I psyched myself into having a good time or at least into convincing Kai that I was enjoying this fiasco.

I followed the same route by the wall and as expected, Kai

NINETEEN: WYATT

was looking in my direction and blew out a breath upon seeing me. I made my way back to him, closing my eyes and taking a deep breath every single time someone bumped into me.

"Are sure you're okay?" he asked the moment I returned.

"I'm fine, please don't worry about me. This'll be fun."

"Ladies and gentlemen, give it up for Chasing Thunder," the announcer's voice boomed from the overhead surround system. One by one the members of the alternative rock band walked on stage to the cheering of the crowd. The drummer was first, followed by the keyboard player then the bassist. Finally, the lead singer walked out and the cheers morphed into a roar when he picked up the guitar and took center stage. I'd heard of the band from Avery and Elizabeth and was surprised that Kai knew the band too. I wasn't going to admit to anyone that I listened to their newest album earlier today.

"Who's ready to rock and roll?" the lead vocalist asked the raucous crowd.

A chorus of *Yeah!* reverberated through the crowd and the lights began to dim. Glow-in-the-dark necklaces and glow-sticks glimmered and floated like fireflies in the darkroom.

The drummer hit his drumsticks together. "Three, two one..."

The intro to their most recent song began thumping, each beat pounding through the speakers from all corners of the theater. The red and yellow lights coming from the stage synced with the music's tempo and smoke appeared in front of the stage.

Everyone, including Kai, danced to the beat causing bodies to bump into me from all sides. I realized too late that I was in the middle of a mosh pit with overzealous fans bouncing off each other. The room began closing in with all four corners shrinking while music vibrated my bones. The *rat-a-tat-tat* from gunfire replaced the staccato drumming and the noise of the screaming fans was replaced with the howls of agony and pain coming from my fellow Marines.

I should have said no. I never should have come here.

Another body slammed into me and with my weakening legs, I stumbled. Kneeling on the floor, I closed my eyes and placed my hands to my ears to muffle the sounds of sorrow bouncing off the walls.

Oh my god.
Not now.
Not here, in front of everyone.
Not in front of Kai.

I was rocking my body back and forth when a familiar voice called out my name.

"Wyatt, open your eyes," the voice shouted. Its owner was so close I felt his breath on my hand that was covering my ear. "Wyatt," he repeated.

Slowly, I opened my eyes only to see twitching burnt limbs bathed in fire.

A hand touched my chin pulling my face up. "Wyatt, it's me. Just look at me and nothing else," he ordered.

Unable to utter a single word, I nodded *yes*, repeatedly.

"Let's get out of here okay? Just listen to my voice and nothing else," the man ordered.

I nodded once again, accepting his hand so he could lead me out of the carnage.

We stood up, my hand gripping his like he was my savior. We navigated the maze of dead soldiers. I was rattled by every bump. I rolled my fist up, preparing to strike out at anybody ready for combat.

NINETEEN: WYATT

"Wyatt, we're almost out. Just listen to my voice." He squeezed my hand which made me focus on his warm eyes. Keeping me in the moment.

Our pace increasing, I let him lead me, not caring where as long as it was somewhere else.

He opened a door and the cool breeze caressed my face when we stepped outside. Even though the noises were faint, I hadn't completely sobered up and my heart continued to thump painfully. The noises were gone, but the thumping of my own heart continued.

"Are you okay?" the man asked. "Take some deep breaths."

I closed my eyes and inhaled deeply. When I opened them again I was staring into the worried eyes of Kai. The realization of what just happened hit me so hard it hurt to breathe. "I need to go," I said in a total panic. I fished my keys out of my pocket and headed across the street to my truck.

"No! You can't drive like this, let's walk a little until you feel better," he pleaded.

I huffed out a breath, knowing I would never be better. "I'm fine. I need to go home."

"Okay, let's get out of here," Kai said as he followed me.

"No, Kai, I wanna go alone," I insisted.

"Wyatt, I don't mind. I'll go with you, just until you're home."

"Kai!" I yelled, facing him.

He flinched and backed off a bit and I felt guilty for raising my voice at him. "I need to go," I ran the last few feet to my truck and jumped in. I spared a glance in my rear-view mirror when I started the engine. Kai was standing where I had left him, watching me drive away. My heart broke at seeing him that way, but my desire to run away was stronger. I swallowed around the massive lump of despair in my throat, "I'm sorry,

Kai."

Twenty: Kai

And Scars

I banged on Wyatt's door hard enough that it rattled the small glass window next to it. "Wyatt, open up! I know you can hear me." I walked around the patio to peek in one of his windows. Bringing my hand to my forehead, I shielded my eyes and looked in when my call went unanswered. Even though he told me he needed to be alone, I followed him anyway because I saw that haunted look in his eyes. "Wyatt, open up," I repeated. When still there was no answer, I walked around to the other side of the patio to peer inside another window and that was when I saw him.

He was sitting on the floor with his back against the door. His head hung low between his bent legs while both of his arms were resting on his knees.

"Wyatt, please let me in?" I said after tapping on the window, trying to get his attention.

"Go away. I just want to be alone," he finally answered.

"I'm not going anywhere until you talk to me." I walked toward the door hoping he'd let me in. When it didn't open, I sat down with my back against the door knowing he was on the other side of it and imagining that our backs were touching. I wanted to be as close as I could. I couldn't stay away from him even if I tried. We sat there for a while in silence. If I closed my eyes and listened close enough, I could hear his breathing.

"There's nothing here for you, Kai. Just fucking go away," he demanded, breaking the silence.

"I'll be right here," I whispered before my head thudded softly against the door. *You can't save him. He's not going to get better.* I should know better than to hope that people could change. I should've learned my lesson from Noah. I stuck around for three and a half years thinking that he'd change. In the end, it wasn't enough.

* * *

"This isn't healthy Kai," my cousin Mikaela said after we sat down on our favorite beach.

I tucked my toes into the white sand and stared at the aquamarine water which appeared bluer from the absence of clouds in the sky. The high noon sun blazing over the coconut trees cast shadows and gave us shade. Many locals were paddling in the water, sitting on their boards, and waiting for the perfect wave to ride. I watched some kids who were building sandcastles ten feet from the surf with their parents while they laughed and giggled. "He's been under a lot of stress lately, you know. He wasn't always like that," I explained.

She twisted to eye me over her shoulder, waiting for me to meet her gaze. "Remember when I told ya that I hoped we wouldn't be having this conversation a year from now?"

I focused my attention on the bright boards floating in the ocean, remembering that conversation as if it were yesterday. I could feel

TWENTY: KAI

her watching me, but I was afraid to look back and see the judgment in her eyes. Or worse, the pity. My eyes burned, my vision blurred and I looked up to the sky and closed my eyes in a lame attempt to stop the tears from forming.

The sand beneath us shifted when Mikaela moved closer and rested her head on my shoulder. "I know how much you love Noah, but calling you worthless and making you feel guilty for spending time with your ohana isn't love"

We sat in silence, staring at the water while our hands absently played with the sand.

"Can I ask you something? And you can tell me to mind my own business, but I really want to know," she asked before pausing a moment.

I held my breath, anticipating her question.

"Why are you still with him?" she continued.

I released the breath I was holding and asked myself the same question. Why do I stay? I loved Noah and I knew he loved me too, but something changed in him after he failed his first attempt to be a Navy SEAL. Then he got worse after his parent's divorce. "I keep thinking he'll go back to his old self." Surprised that I said those words out loud, I continued, "I'm all he's got here."

"Oh, Kai, those aren't the right reasons—"

"Don't say that. Please don't say that." I buried my face between my knees. I knew those weren't reasons to stay in a relationship, but I didn't want to hear it. "I know how ridiculous that sounds, but I don't know what you want me to say."

"It doesn't matter what I want to hear from you, Kai. It's what you want for yourself," she explained. "You're the smartest person I know, the first person in our family to graduate from college and you did it while working your ass off. You deserve so much better than him."

"I don't want to have this conversation with you."

"Trust me, Kai, I don't either. But I'm not gonna sit back and watch you hurt. You can hate me, but I'll never stop looking out for you. Like when you looked out for me when both of my parents died."

* * *

Shuffling noises surprised me and I readjusted to check behind me. The door unlocked and Wyatt stood in the doorway. I wiped my cheeks with the back of my hand and looked up into his red-rimmed eyes. He offered me a hand which I gladly accepted. He pulled me into his arms and guided me into the house before kicking the door closed behind us.

He hugged me tightly, "I'm so sorry, Kai. I'm so fucking sorry." He kissed the top of my head uttering the same phrase over and over again.

Thankful that Wyatt had finally let me inside, I nodded because I didn't want to push him too fast. A war of emotions played in my head, hesitation was paralyzing my whole body. I wanted to be there for him, to let him know that I will always be with him, but I was scared too.

Wyatt lifted my chin when I didn't speak and looked into my eyes. "Please say something," he pleaded.

Moment of truth. I had to tell him. I'd never told this to anyone, but Wyatt needed to know. "I understand your pain and your struggles, and you might not be ready to share them with me, but walking away like that hurt. It took me to a place that I never wanted to revisit."

TWENTY: KAI

I told Wyatt about my past relationship and how violent it became toward the end of Noah and me.

"Oh my god, I had no idea," Wyatt said afterward, pulling me back into his embrace. His body was shaking. "I will never hurt you like that. I'm not that guy. I promise."

If there was one thing I learned from my relationship with Noah was you couldn't promise something like that, but I wouldn't punish Wyatt with Noah's mistakes. I cupped his face and nodded. "Thank you." I lowered his head so I could kiss his forehead.

He led me to his bedroom and we rested on top of the bed. "Would you spend the night?" he asked as I continued to caress his abs through his shirt, tracing each firm muscle one bulge at a time. I rested my cheek on his chest, feeling his heart beating. Call me insane, but I could've sworn it matched mine. Pulse by pulse, drum by drum.

I'd spend a lifetime if you'd let me was what I wanted to say. Instead, I settled on, "Yes." A simple three-letter word packed with implications, but that's a worry for a different day. For now, I surrendered to my need to stay close to this complicated man.

Wyatt blew out a breath I didn't realize he was holding when he drew me tighter to his body and kissed the top of my head. "Big spoon or little spoon?" he asked, still subdued.

"I was thinking fork." That earned me a chuckle which sent shockwaves to my core.

"How do you do that?" Wyatt asked with a smirk.

"Do what?"

"Make things better."

"I don't know," I shrugged because that was the truth.

Lying this close to him with our clothes on, doing nothing

but holding each other was the strongest connection I'd ever had.

"What's it feel like living in Hawai'i? Is it like being on vacation all the time?" he asked, playing with my hair.

"It's the opposite actually," I answered, enjoying his soft caress near my temple.

"Really? How's that even possible? You're surrounded by paradise!"

Shrugging, I angled my head so I could study his features in the dark. "Don't get me wrong, it's gorgeous, but Oahu is a small island. You run out of things to do fairly quickly."

"Still though, I'd love to go one day."

"Wait, you've never been to Hawai'i?" My eyes widened and I was unsure why that shocked me. "It's only a five-hour flight from Seattle."

"I know. Just never had a reason to. I joined the military after college and we never really went anywhere when I was younger."

"You'll like it. There's this amazing beach half a mile from where I lived, and it's the perfect place to surf and the food is amazing."

"Local food?"

"The only kind we like. There's this food truck called Aloha Joe, and I swear they serve the best loco-moco in Hawai'i. It's so popular he sells out by noon."

"Just like the muffins in the café."

"Exactly like that," I agreed.

We stayed in silence for a while, but it was welcomed this time. It gave Wyatt the opportunity to work on whatever was troubling him.

"Thank you for coming after me. I'm sorry it ruined our

TWENTY: KAI

evening," he took my hand resting on his chest and kissed it before placing it back where it was.

"I'd rather be here with you than anywhere else," I admitted. "Wyatt?" I asked, hoping he wouldn't dodge my next question.

"Yeah?"

"Who is Jim?"

He was quiet for a while, but he eventually spoke. "He was a friend of mine. We were on the same team when we were overseas."

"What happened to him?"

"An IED exploded near us, missing me, but not him, unfortunately. It'll be four years next week. He was a great man."

"I'm so sorry, Wyatt. Is that why you get these attacks?" I turned to face him and I wiped the tears that started to fall once again from his eyes.

"Yes. He was like a younger brother and his parents treated me like another son."

"Do you see them often?"

"Not since Jim's service. I don't know if I could ever look them in the eye again. I had promised to take care of Jim, but I failed."

"Wyatt, it wasn't your fault." I touched the scar on his eyebrow and wondered if it had been from the military.

"I got that from the first day of boot camp," he explained as if he was able to read my wandering mind. "Why don't we crawl under the covers and call it a night?"

I huffed out a breath and I figured this was his attempt to change the subject. As frustrated as I was, I agreed.

Twenty-One: Kai

We Hide

The windshield wipers were working double duty to keep up with the heavy Hawaiian rainfall as we navigated the winding road to our ohana's home. It had become more difficult to see the road because of the headlights reflecting off the rainwater. This one-lane road had been nicknamed Jinx Way because of the number of accidents that happened here year after year. It already recorded its fourteenth accident this year alone and it was only February. The lightning and thunder had stopped, but the torrential rain had been pouring continuously for a couple of days. A typical occurrence in Hawai'i during the months of January to March.

I offered to drive since I was familiar with the road and had driven it in this condition.

"I can't believe he hit you?" Lei was still fuming miles after we'd left the rental house I shared with Noah. She reached to touch my chin and I grimaced from the contact. "Does it hurt?" she asked.

I used the rear-view mirror to check my reflection. My left lower lip had a cut and the red skin around it was turning black and purple. "I'll be fine. Thanks for getting me."

"Of course I'd come get you. What are you gonna do now?"

TWENTY-ONE: KAI

"I don't know."

The winding local road ended, and we merged onto the interstate. I found myself relaxing a little.

The deafening crunch of metal on metal caused my Jeep to veer into another lane. Lei screamed mixed with the blare of a horn when blinding yellow lights skidded toward her. I quickly turned my steering wheel to the left, trying to avoid whatever was about to hit us.

I blinked when cold water trickled down my face. My head was killing me and it took a couple of seconds of staring at the powder-covered dash and the depleted airbag before I realized what had happened.

"Lei?" I called out. My own voice sounded distant through my ringing ears and panic took over my entire body. Ignoring my pain, I attempted to push the thick fabric of the airbag and powder-covered glass aside so I could release my seatbelt. "Lei?" I screamed when she didn't answer.

In the distance, I could hear the wail of sirens echoing through the pitter-patter of rain. I wasn't a religious person, but at the moment, I was willing to pray to any god who would listen. Please let her be okay. Take me instead. *I choked on a sob. My mouth was full of spit and blood, causing me to cough.*

"Kai?" her weak voice answered.

I'd never been more thankful to hear my name. "Lei, thank god! Thank god!"

"I'm stuck," she cried.

"Just hang in there, help is coming."

Lights flashed on us and the paramedics began to assess our situation.

"Are you okay? What's your name? Do you know where you are?" someone asked Lei a series of questions.

"Do you know how you got here?" someone asked me while flashing a light in my eyes. "Have you been drinking?" he continued.

"What? No!" I objected. I knew why they had to ask that question, but being accused of driving while drunk didn't sit well with me. "I... I don't know what happened..."

A firefighter opened the doors using the Jaws of Life to get us out of the car and onto a stretcher. "We're taking both of you to the hospital. Is there someone we can call for you?"

"Yes, please call my parents." I gave the officer their number.

* * *

I was startled by the vibrations coming from the nightstand and since my phone was always on silent, it had to be Wyatt's. The buzzing continued and the light from its screen illuminated the darkroom. I'd been up for a while because last night's concert had brought to the surface the tragic events from the night of the accident.

"Who the fuck's calling this early?" Wyatt groaned, reaching for his cell.

I was able to peek at his phone before he answered, and it was only a quarter past five in the morning and the caller ID read Elizabeth. A phone call before sunrise was never a good thing.

"Someone better be dying, the sun isn't even up yet," he said, skipping all the pleasantries. He listened for a while, and I could hear the caller chattering in the background before he continued, "Why do we keep Roy? He's so un-fucking-unreliable."

TWENTY-ONE: KAI

Another silence and Wyatt sat up and pinched the bridge of his nose with two fingers. "I'll figure something out. Thanks for letting me know."

He threw his cell on the foot of the bed and flopped back with a heavy sigh.

"Remind me to never call before sunrise," I teased.

"One of the guys called out sick again and we're already running the charters with skeleton crews. I'm going to have to figure out who can help me with this last-minute request. Goddamn it."

"Is he okay?" I asked, hoping it wasn't the wrong question to ask.

"I don't know. He just called Elizabeth to let her know that he'll miss the sailing this morning. I'm firing his ass when I see him next time," he fumed.

"Are you sure you wanna do that? You don't even know why he called out," I blurted before I was able to stop my big mouth from speaking.

Wyatt rolled to his side and looked at me, "What?"

"I'm just saying maybe you should find out why he couldn't make it to work," I held my breath ready to argue. I knew I shouldn't poke the bear this early, especially in the middle of a work crisis, but people should be given a second chance. People make mistakes, and that doesn't mean they're bad people. That simple thought made me feel like a fraud. How was I willing to give others a second chance when I couldn't give myself the same courtesy? *'It was an accident, Kai, it's not your fault,'* said my ma's voice in the head.

"Are you always this nice? You always see the good in people. But you're right about giving him another chance. Everyone deserves a second chance. I was just upset is all." He kissed my forehead, something I noticed he did a lot.

"What are you gonna do?" I asked.

"We have a couple of guys that we keep for situations like this, I'll call them."

"What kind of help do you need?"

"With everything to tell you the truth. Stuff like helping me launch the boat, guiding me out of the harbor, securing the anchor, helping me serve snacks and just another person on board in case of emergencies," Wyatt explained.

"Could I help?"

Wyatt looked at me perhaps wondering if I was kidding, but I wasn't. I grew up in Hawai'i and had experience chartering boats catered to tourists. "Do you know anything about charter boats?"

I rolled my eyes at him, "That's what we do back home whenever we need extra money. I used to do it during college breaks, the tips were great."

Wyatt's eyes widened. "Are you for real?" His excitement was evident.

"Yes, are we sailing a sailboat or a catamaran?"

"Catamaran."

"Piece of cake."

Twenty-Two: Wyatt

Orcas Mate For Life

Kai started opening each of the boat's compartments to check the number of life vests before continuing with his pre-sailing checklist on his clipboard while walking around the boat. *This could be us, this could be our future.* The thought caused my chest to tighten, threatening a different kind of anxiety from the ones associated with Jim's death.

"Everything checks out and we're ready to board Captain Miller," Kai teased, giving me a hand salute.

I gave him a thumbs up since my heart was lodged in my throat, preventing me from saying anything.

He turned his attention to the line of tourists scheduled for the tour and greeted them, enchanting everyone with his charm. "Alright, folks, ready to have some fun?" he asked.

"Yeah!" the group answered in unison, matching his eagerness.

Kai began to check in our passengers still holding the clipboard and handing them a sheet of safety instructions. "We'll go over these before we head out," he told everyone.

It quickly became clear how natural Kai was around tourists

fifteen minutes into our sailing. He answered questions from passengers about safety and I could be biased, but this sailing was the smoothest I'd had in a very long time.

I had been nervous about how this would turn out. Although I was excited to hang out with him all morning, I was hesitant after the night we had for two reasons. First was the safety of our passengers, and second, was how our situation would affect the dynamics of working together.

"Northwest, about a mile from the port side." Kai handed me the pair of binoculars and pointed me in that direction. "Are those Orcas?"

"Sure are!" I handed the binoculars back to him before grabbing my radio to let our passengers know to look in that direction.

A collective gasp of excitement was followed by bright flashes and mechanical clicks when the passengers started taking pictures and videos of the amazing killer whales.

"Is it okay if I check it out?" Kai asked, "I've never seen orcas before. We have a lot of spinner dolphins and humpback whales in Hawai'i, but not killer whales."

Wanting to experience this with him, I turned off the engine. "Let's drop the anchor so we can enjoy it."

Kai's face lit up like a Christmas tree and if we weren't surrounded by strangers, I would have kissed him. I didn't have any problem with public displays of affection, but we were at work and this was business. I wasn't about to mix business with pleasure. "Are you sure?"

I gave him a wink and he helped me drop anchor.

"Oh my gosh, they're swimming toward us," a woman shrieked from the back of the boat. She was pointing at the playful pod which was putting on a spectacular show for the

TWENTY-TWO: WYATT

guests.

Even though we were the invaders in the pod's natural habitat, the orcas managed to swim closer to the catamaran.

A sheen of black and white bobbed around the surface, blowing air out of their blowholes. The orcas seemed to love the attention and praise and began to inch even closer to one of the hulls.

"This is so cool," Kai said. "I can't believe how close they are, I can almost touch them."

His excitement was contagious, I dared anyone to spend time with him and not be put in a better mood.

"They're amazing." I wrapped my arms around him and kissed the side of his head, breaking my own rule about mixing business and pleasure.

"I told you they're together," a woman standing next to us said to her friend. "It was obvious the way the captain was looking at him," she whispered.

A flush of color crept up Kai's neck to his face. He turned around and buried his face in my chest to hide his blushing. We hadn't spoken about labels, but I knew he felt the same about me. The way he looked at me spoke the words he hadn't.

"You guys look great together," the other woman said.

I was clueless about how to respond to her statement, so I just let it hang there.

"Did you know that killer whales mate for life?" I whispered to Kai.

He looked up from my chest and said, "No, they don't. They're social and live as one unit, but they don't mate for life," he argued.

I knew that, but I wanted to believe they did. "Maybe they do once they find *the one*, you know," I explained, hoping no one heard my ridiculous theory.

The intense look on Kai's face was back and for a moment, I thought he'd kiss me. Instead, he went along with my theory, "I like that idea. Anything is possible once you find *the one*."

The stark reminder of what I couldn't have whenever I looked at Kai was slowly being replaced by hope. Maybe, just maybe, I could be like everybody else.

Loved.

"What's on your mind, Lance Corporal?" Kai's question took me out of the hole I often dug for myself whenever a part of me dared to be happy.

I hadn't realized that I'd been staring at him. "Do you wanna go camping after this?" I asked.

"Like overnight? Don't you have to work tomorrow?" Kai asked.

"I have some days off coming up, and I'd like to take you camping. If you're into that sort of thing and—"

"I'd love to," he answered, saving me from my rambling.

"Great! I know an awesome place."

Twenty-Three: Kai

Semper Fi

Following Wyatt down the wooded trail, I couldn't take my eyes off his muscular butt and the way it was held snug by his tight, camo-colored shorts. We'd alternated taking the lead on the hike and I was more than happy to follow him. I was utterly mesmerized by this rugged man. I'd become quite enamored with him these past couple of weeks. We'd almost completed a six-mile hike on day one of our camping adventures and were heading back to the campsite we'd set up next to a small tranquil lake that he'd known about from hiking with Avery, Elizabeth, and Elijah.

"Hotter than I thought it'd be," he said as we approached the campsite.

"Seriously, especially for a temperate rainforest."

We'd taken the ferry from the islands to Port Angeles, and had driven Wyatt's truck through the town of Forks, where they'd filmed the *Twilight* series. After a short pitstop, we headed into the Olympic National Park's rainforest. Once we found the trailhead and loaded up our gear into manageable backpacks, we began the journey to the secluded lake which was nearly two miles into the woods. Because of the terrain, the lake offered privacy. We'd set up our large tent about fifteen yards from the shore of the small lake. The tent slept four easily, so there was plenty of room for us to spread out with our gear.

I was extremely excited that it was just the two of us camped out at this beautiful spot.

I watched as Wyatt stripped his tight t-shirt off and hung it on a nearby shrub. I watched the sweat trailing down between his pecs, glistening in the sunlight. He looked hotter than I remembered. The Marine Corps insignia tattoo on his right pec stood out from the moist flesh. I swallowed hard and released a heavy breath. I was full of desire and wanted to trace his tattoo with my tongue. He also had a smaller tattoo with the Marine's mantra, Semper Fi, written on his left side in black ink. There was certainly no doubt that he was a Marine. At six foot four and two hundred thirty pounds of raw muscle, he was a sight to behold.

"Wanna cool off Kai?" He glanced at the shimmering lake and then back to me with a raised eyebrow.

It was about half an hour before we'd be losing our sun, so I figured we could cool down and bathe at the same time. "Sure, I'll grab the bar of soap. We can kill two birds, sorta thing."

I headed to the tent, unzipped it, and crawled in so I could dig through my duffel bag for soap and a couple of towels. My fingers touched the lube and condoms I'd slipped into the bag and set those aside, hoping they'd get used soon. When I exited the tent, I noticed a naked Wyatt already standing at the edge of the water with his back to me. His strong muscled back with a perfect V-shape was also moist with sweat. His round chiseled ass cheeks were glowing white in the dimming light. He had a nice tan from long days on the boats, but that

TWENTY-THREE: KAI

gorgeous ass of his was a beacon, begging me to salivate as I caught my breath.

"Hey soldier," I said, letting him know I was behind him.

He didn't bother to turn around. "Staring at my ass, are ya?" he laughed, still looking out at the lake.

"Can't help it. You're quite the specimen," I admitted.

He turned around and stood in front of me with no attempt at modesty in his movements. His large cock was on full display. I hadn't forgotten about that asset and seeing it again made me horny. It had taken me a day or two to recover after having enjoyed it inside me the last time, and I had high hopes he'd be sharing it again on the camping trip. It was well worth a little discomfort, and I was hoping for the opportunity to get used to his girth.

"Care to slip out of those shorts and join me?"

He didn't have to ask twice. I yanked my tee off and then pulled my shorts and briefs off in one swift movement. Wyatt's eyes never left my body as I stripped down to nothing, my dick swelling from remembering how good his cock felt in me the last time.

"Someone's excited about something," he said, staring directly at my burgeoning erection.

"Better enjoy it before it hits that cold water," I laughed, knowing I was a grower and not a shower.

"Maybe that won't happen on this swim?" he snarled, making my cock even harder to hide. "Come here, sexy. Let me check that out."

I walked over and stood wantonly in front of him as he smiled. He examined my nakedness, running his warm hands over my chest.

"You have amazing skin. The color is incredible and you're

so smooth and flawless, even with this scar," he whispered after trailing a finger on my scar. He placed his hand to a noticeable scar on his stomach, trying to suddenly hide it.

I grabbed the hand that was covering the scar and pulled it away. I replaced it with my own and traced the outline of the old wound. I slowly moved my other hand across his abs to his side where there were two similar scars. I knew those were from Afghanistan. I also knew he wouldn't talk about them or the war, but I thought they added to his overall sexiness.

"I love how you look. I'm sorry if they're painful reminders, but I think you're perfect Wyatt." I turned my face up to his, where I found him studying me, searching my eyes for the reason that I could believe he was perfect.

"Thank you for that," he whispered, relaxing his hands to his side, becoming comfortable with my caresses.

"I'm not lying, you are perfect… for me."

He pulled me into a tight embrace and held me in his arms. I instinctively brought my face to his chest and let myself be absorbed into his massive body.

"You're perfect, but also sweaty, mister!" I laughed, pushing myself away.

He grabbed me around the waist and picked me up, tossing me over his shoulder like I was a sack of potatoes. I struggled to get out of his grip, but it was impossible because he was so strong. Wyatt walked to the edge of the water, still holding me and in full control.

"Now, what was that? I don't quite remember exactly what you said. How about you try that again," he threatened, his grip on my waist even tighter.

"Nothing, I said nothing. I'm pleading the fifth," I laughed, trying to get out of his arms and back on land.

TWENTY-THREE: KAI

"Too late, gorgeous." And with that, he tossed me into the water.

I came up spitting water and tried to find my footing. But before I could, he had dived in and had me back in his arms. He held me in his embrace and I realized he was standing even though I couldn't feel the bottom of the lake. Wyatt was six inches taller than me. I felt protected but also knew he could break me in two if he wanted.

He continued to hold me and brought his mouth down to mine, slipping his tongue in between my lips. He was powerful and gentle at the same time. His mouth continued to probe mine when our kiss became hard and passionate. I knew he wanted me, wanted to possess all of me.

I felt the pressure of his swelling cock against my hip, more evidence that he was intent on fulfilling our desires.

"I was going to swim and cool off, but that isn't happening," he admitted, nestling his face in my neck. "Where's that soap?"

I motioned for the edge of the water, and he started walking there, still holding me in his embrace.

"Really?" I asked, being carried through the water like no weight was on him.

He tossed me into the lake again and swam for the shore to grab the soap. I chased after him, grabbing an ankle and pulling him under the water with me. We joined again and kissed. Both of us were hard as rocks and were rubbing ourselves over one another's bodies.

"Let's clean up, I need you in me now," I growled.

I grabbed the soap and joined him. Both of us were standing in knee-deep water when I came up behind him and moved the bar of soap over his back and neck, massaging him as I went. He patiently stood while my hands traveled down to his firm ass and began to move my fingers along the crack, lathering and exploring. He tensed up as my finger slid near his hole.

"Relax," I whispered, holding my finger near his hole to see if he'd allow it.

"You can wash it, but no loitering, if you get my drift."

"Oh yeah? I get your drift alright. Let's save the probing for me," I growled, rubbing my erection against his butt cheeks and teasing him even more.

I came around to his front and handed him the bar so I could get a good lather built up in my hands. After some serious suds had foamed up, I reached for his semi-erect shaft. Holding his nuts with one hand, I rubbed up and down his shaft with my other soapy hand. He stood taller and arched, his head back as he enjoyed the personal massage.

"The last time you massaged me, we ended up—you know," he winked.

"I know," I murmured, increasing my grip on his thick cock, massaging his balls gently with my fingers.

I took the soap back and cleaned his chest and face but avoided his eyes, so he could watch me clean his incredibly sexy body. I felt powerful as I washed him and held his hardness in my hand.

"My turn," I said, turning away, inviting him to start with my back and hungry ass.

Wyatt ran the soap over my shoulders and down my spine, building up a good foam before moving the bar to the curve of my ass. I pushed my cheeks back to him, encouraging him to move it lower. He gently ran the bar under my opening and toward my balls, hanging below a throbbing cock. His fingers swirled around my pucker, gently pushing into my resistance,

TWENTY-THREE: KAI

and then breaking through. I gasped as a soapy finger made its way into me. He had one hand on my shoulder, holding me in place as the other hand kept darting in and out of me.

"Fuck... that feels too amazing, but be careful, I'm so fucking horny, and I don't wanna shoot like this," I moaned, driving my ass into him.

He bent his knees lower and slipped his cock in between my butt cheeks, holding my hips as he slid his soapy tool back and forth, driving me crazy. I reached my arms back and wrapped them around his neck as he held me tight, my back pressed against his chest as he continued to hump my ass. I felt the head of his dick hitting the back of my nut sack as his long cock slid between my thighs.

"I want to be inside you, right now," he murmured, heat in his voice.

I turned around and placed my hands on his strong hips and kissed him, craving the erection that was stabbing my stomach. We stood there exploring each other in a lake in the middle of the woods. The sun had dipped behind a stand of trees and twilight had taken over. Wyatt moved me to deeper water, still holding me as the soap rinsed away from our skin. He ran the bar over my hair, getting an easy shampoo-like lather going.

"This is a Marine bath and shampoo. We use a bar of soap for everything, hope it won't ruin your usual routine," he stated, rubbing my head and being careful to keep the soap out of my eyes.

"Whatever you say, boss. Just don't forget my cock. Junior needs a rub and tug too."

"Oh, don't you worry your pretty little face about that, I'll be tugging on that soon enough," he rumbled before bringing his lips down to mine.

We finished rinsing by dipping into the water, its coolness doing nothing to diminish our aching needs. He grabbed my hand and led me to the tent, neither of us saying a word as we walked the twenty yards or so. His huge cock was swinging back and forth, keeping rhythm with his pace.

We slipped into the tent, and I laid on my stomach, tempting him to lay on top of me so I could feel the delicious weight of his massive body. He fulfilled my unspoken command when laid on me. Our bodies fit as if we were molded for each other. I welcomed the pressure when he ground his hips against my eager butt. His cock pressed against my lower back, drawing an imaginary line against my skin.

Wyatt placed his mouth on the back of my neck and nibbled on sensitive flesh when ground harder. He was driving me insane. I felt like an animal being mounted from behind and was aroused beyond belief.

"I know we should do some more foreplay, but I need to feel that cock inside me," I begged, arching my ass up higher, consumed with desire.

"Lube?" he grunted in my ear.

Knowing I was about to get my wish, I felt for the lube and a condom that I'd left by my duffel earlier, realizing how smart I'd been in hindsight. I felt him lift his weight off me as he came to his knees. He turned on the LED lantern before opening the foil packet. I looked over my shoulder to watch him roll the condom on, slather some lube over his swollen shaft, and finally moved his fingers to my waiting hole.

Wyatt's chest touched my back, he'd slid a bit lower so that his cock's head was just below my waiting entrance before he pressed the tip up and against my opening.

"Is this what you want?" his gravelly voice asked. "You think

TWENTY-THREE: KAI

you can handle this again? I plan to do it slow, is that ok?"

"Whatever you want Wyatt, I just need you inside me."

"Relax, let me play with you awhile," he whispered, moving his lubed-up cock closer to my hole, his hips gyrating as he moved over a very horny and smooth ass. "This what you like? You like when I tease your hole with my tip?" He had his face buried against my neck where his teeth grazed my skin with his hot breath escaping as he pumped his dick into my crack.

"Put it in," I moaned.

"Not so fast, baby. Let me take my sweet time. You're so fucking hot, I want to enjoy every single moment. Every. Single. Inch. When I penetrate you."

He was driving me crazy. The combination of his weight dominating me, my dick rubbing against the sleeping bag, and his husky voice, delirious in my ear, had me ready to blow my load.

"Come on Wyatt, no more teasing, I need your cock now... please," I begged again, pushing my ass cheeks up hard against his very large dick. I lifted and positioned his cock against my entrance. "Yes... put it in... that's it, I need it now." He had me so worked up, I couldn't stand it anymore. So I pushed my ass up and felt his tip slide into my lubed ass.

"Fuck, you're tight," he moaned, applying a little more pressure. He slowly pushed in so I could adjust and welcome more of his inches.

I relaxed as he sunk deeper into me and began to move. My erection continued to grind against the sleeping bag.

Wyatt was moaning in my ear, his hum low and sexy as he conveyed his pleasure at being inside me. "I'm going to enjoy this, let me know if it's too much."

I let him know how I felt about that statement by arching

my back and placing my ass squarely into his firing zone.

"Roll over Kai," he stated, pulling himself out. "I want to see your eyes when I'm inside you."

I felt my heart swell at his request and rolled onto my back. Wyatt brought his mouth down to my cock and took it deep in one move, sucking me and letting me fill his mouth. He held me in, while he deep throated me. I was smaller than him but still, deep throating seven inches wasn't exactly easy.

"Mmmppfff," he mumbled as his hands traced my abs before gripping my hips and pulling me deeper into his mouth. He used his brute strength to move my hips, making my throbbing dick fuck his face. I focused on him, the muscles in his arms bulging when he lifted me off the sleeping bag and into him with ease. He was concentrating on milking me dry when I felt that tightness in my sack. I knew I'd better be careful because I was hot and ready to shoot. I tapped his arm.

"Easy fella, I'm gonna bust if you're not careful and I want you back inside me when I shoot."

I lifted my legs by holding the back of my knees, exposing myself to Wyatt to encourage him to enter me again. He took the hint and grabbed my ankles with one hand and guided his dick back to my waiting hole. I closed my eyes and gritted my teeth when his cock slowly reentered me. Wyatt adjusted my feet to his shoulders, nuzzling his chin against it before leaning forward, powering his way into me again. With each stroke, he thrust deeper and harder. I stared up at him and he was grinning with excitement, his eyes rolled from the pleasure of being joined. He leaned forward so his soft lips could capture mine and his tongue darted in and out. I cupped his face so I could feel the roughness of his stubble. Our eyes gazed upon each other as our rhythm came together in our scintillating

TWENTY-THREE: KAI

act. I welcomed him and felt his affection as his masculinity took me away to a dream-like place. I'd never felt so connected with another human being.

"You're amazing. You feel so good when I'm in you like this," he admitted, a mischievous glint in his eye when he moved in and out with fluid pumps of his hips.

His admission made my dick throb. "Your cock feels so good. I need it bad. Can you give it to me harder and faster now?" I begged.

"You want it hard? How hard?" he asked.

"I want you to make me feel it, shoot your load deep into me."

"Ok, since you asked so sweetly," he moaned, his eyes sparkling at the invitation. "Hope you're ready for this."

Wyatt leaned back and moved my legs off his shoulders and grabbed my ankles again, kissing them in between thrusts. He spread my legs apart as wide as I could handle and looked down to my hole. He slowly pulled out and thrust back in, gasping with each thrust. I moved my hands above my head to expose myself to him.

The pace was increasing, and his eyes darted between my face and himself pumping into my ass. My hole was wide open, and I felt the warm sensation of euphoria rising inside of me while he continued to rub against my prostate. I grabbed my dick and stroked it in time with him filling me up. My precum was leaking and I knew I was close.

"That's it… faster, I'm getting there," I groaned, fisting my cock harder.

Wyatt moaned his passion and pumped into me faster, hitting my hot spot just like I wanted. The shivers of excitement gripped my insides as the stimulation had me hurdling closer to that magical burst of release.

Gripping my ass cheeks, he plunged harder into me, controlling his lifts to meet my eager hole and drive me crazy from the electric currents surging through my groin.

We both stared at each other in lust, the pleasure building. I stroked harder, he plunged deeper. I could tell he was close when he closed his eyes and I expected he'd be shooting his pleasure any minute now. His eyes popped open just as I felt my load churning forth. My asshole clamped down around him, milking him and making him finish with me.

"Oh my... fuck!" he yelled.

All I could do was let my eyes roll back into my head as I lost myself in the most incredible orgasm I'd ever experienced. I opened my mouth, unable to make any noise because everything around me stopped. My heart lurched and my lungs locked.

"Yes! Yes! Fuck that's good," he moaned, his dick emptying its load.

Wyatt fell forward onto me, forcing me to exhale incoherent words, just as the last bit of cum left my dick. I wrapped my arms and legs around him, pulling him into me.

"I had no idea it could be so good," he said, snuggling into my neck, kissing me gently.

"Me either," I admitted.

Twenty-Four: Wyatt

That's A Worry For Tomorrow

The ferry back to Friday Harbor was one of my favorite parts of living in the San Juan Islands. I get to enjoy the scenery without being responsible for sailing the ship. It wasn't like I could captain this behemoth, but the size of this boat dwarfed other sailboats and yachts nearby. The deep blue water shimmered with the sun hitting the waves. The neighboring island's rolling hills were covered with pine trees, and the narrow passages of the Puget Sound could rival the fjords of Norway and New Zealand.

The ferry slowed down to a complete stop and everyone wondered why.

"Why did we stop?" Kai said while looking around.

"I'm not sure, sometimes the ferry stops to let barges or container ships pass ,but I don't see anything."

"Should we go back to the car?"

"Is that a submarine?" one of the passengers asked before I had the chance to answer Kai's question.

I looked to where the passenger was pointing and saw a long black torpedo with a tower containing the periscope. It was glistening as the water cascaded down because it was emerging from the depths. "Look, Kai! That's a submarine."

Kai stood in front of me and I pointed in the direction of the sub while my other hand wrapped around the back of his neck. "Oh my goodness. Like a military submarine?" he asked, after turning to look at me.

"Yes, it is. Our state has one of the largest naval bases and I believe that's one of those Trident Nuclear Subs."

"That is so cool." Kai's eyes glimmered with excitement as if he just opened his favorite present on Christmas Morning. "And I love it when you talk military."

I was falling for Kai, and the more I was with him, the more I wanted to be a better person.

More passengers, including kids, gathered around the broad steel deck where we were standing to get a glimpse of the elusive Trident.

"Tell me more about your family and life in Hawai'i," I said while we drove off the ferry toward home. I knew two things about him so far, he loved to surf, and he was an architect. Desperate to learn more, I continued, "You never talk about them."

Kai's posture became rigid and he pulled his hand that was resting on my leg away. He looked out the window avoiding my stare. Odd, but I'd seen that reaction whenever the topic of his family and life in Hawai'i came up.

"Kai, is everything okay?" Still, with no answer, I began to worry and pulled over to the side of the road. After placing the truck in park, I turned to face him. "What's wrong?" I asked.

Kai played with the hem of his shirt.

I wanted him to open up. "I can tell something's amiss with

TWENTY-FOUR: WYATT

your family. You go silent every time I mention them, and I've seen you screen their calls." I unbuckled my seatbelt and leaned closer to him. "How'd you get that?" I pointed to the scar on his arm.

"I'm fine, let's just keep going," he mumbled.

"No, you're not fine. What's going on?" I hated seeing him distraught. I needed to know what made him upset so I could try to fix it for him. I wanted him to trust me.

"My family hates me," he continued. Tears started cascading down his cheeks.

I was momentarily stunned. "What? How could your family hate you? Talk to me, please? These tears are killing me." I slid across the seat and wrapped my arms around him.

I wasn't the only one who was hurting. After a few minutes of letting him cry, it dawned on me that I was falling in love with Kai. I would do anything to take all his pain away, and that fucking scared the shit out of me.

After his crying subsided, I loosened my hold on him and tilted his head back to look into his eyes. The sparkle I'd come to love had been overtaken by a wave of dark clouds. I was lost. I didn't know what to do or what to say. Helplessness was all I felt.

I gambled and decided to be honest with him about what I felt. I closed the distance between our lips for a soft, sensual kiss. "I love you, Kai, and I hate seeing you like this." I didn't know how this was going to end, but I would worry about it tomorrow.

His eyes widened, but he never looked away, instead he said, "I love you too, Wyatt."

Kai loved me too and that was equally as terrifying and freeing. I'd never been with anyone who treated me with kindness like he did. The way he looked at me like I was the king of the world, made me feel that I was worth something. More than my damaged self. "No one cares for me the way you do. You're always there when I need someone. Sometimes, I think that you're just a dream, a dream that I don't want to wake up from."

"I'll always be here for you," Kai said with conviction.

I believed him.

Twenty-Five: Kai

He Loved Me

Fear. That was the best word I could come up with to describe what I felt when Wyatt told me he loved me. I loved him too, but I'd never been this scared in my life. "I ran away from home because I broke my family," I started.

Wyatt was still looking at me, waiting for me to continue. *If I crumble tonight, will I still be whole tomorrow?* I closed my eyes and began to tell him the reason why I moved away from the only home I'd known.

* * *

Dr. Iwata, the surgeon who operated on Leilani the night after the accident, entered the room and greeted us before taking the seat closest to the computer. She turned to face the examination table where Lei was sitting with her right lower leg, wrapped in plaster. The other had a black brace with a metal rod on either side that matched the bruising on her skin. "How are you, Lei?" she asked after exchanging pleasantries with the rest of us.

"Okay, I guess," a subdued Lei answered, her attention everywhere else but the doctor. She was playing with the cloth wrapped around her thigh and hiding behind her long black hair which hung loosely around her face.

Dr. Iwata lowered the table until it was four feet off the ground and looked between Lei's hair. "Let's get you out of this plaster so we can check, okay?"

Instead of answering, Lei nodded and tucked her hair behind her ears, sorrow painted on her expression. Her eyes were red from crying and had dark bags under them. Gone was the smiling face with eyes illuminated with youth and joy.

My stomach dropped, making me want to vomit because I was the one who caused that look. I wish it had been me who was sitting on that table instead of her. It was all my fault. If I hadn't called her to save my sorry ass, she wouldn't be there. We would never have had that accident.

Dr. Iwata put on a pair of blue vinyl gloves and pulled a pair of scissors from the pocket of her crisp white coat. She started cutting the fabric from Lei's thigh, down to her lower leg. She placed the pair of scissors on the blue-lined metal tray next to the exam table and pulled the plaster cast open. She applied extra force to break the mold of cloth and the chalk-looking material which had hardened to protect Lei's right leg. Gently, she pulled the plaster away, exposing Lei's leg that was covered with patches of four by four white gauze, only they were soaked and covered with dried blood.

"I didn't think you could cut the cast with just scissors," Lei spoke, curiosity in her eyes temporarily replaced the gauntness that had been living in there these past two weeks.

Dr. Iwata chuckled and showed her the mold. "You can't. This is different from a cast. You know the colorful ones? This is just a temporary plaster we put on after surgery. We leave this gap open

TWENTY-FIVE: KAI

and wrap it with bandages," she explained.

Just like earlier, Lei just nodded.

One by one, Dr. Iwata pulled each gauze off and dropped them onto the same metal tray where the scissors were.

A sharp gasp from my mom, followed by Lei's silent tears tugged at my soul when the doctor exposed the long incision that ran from her thigh to her lower knee that had been sewn together with black sutures.

I stood up, went around to the other side of the table, and wrapped an arm around Lei's shoulder. She buried her face in my chest and cried. I rubbed her back and kissed the top of her head to console her. The urge to protect my little sister was stronger than the helplessness and the guilt that I felt.

"It's okay sweetie, it's supposed to look like that. It'll look a lot better once we take the sutures out." Dr. Iwata affirmed, but it wasn't enough to stop Lei from crying. "We'll get some X-rays before we do, okay?" She looked at my parents.

Pa put his arm on Ma who was finally able to hide the agony on her face moments before, and they both nodded.

After carefully getting Lei to a wheelchair, the nurse rolled her out of the room to get an X-ray.

A valve opened and released all the pressure of the past two weeks, and I finally broke down. "It's all my fault. She's suffering because of me." I sat down on the same table where Lei had been. The sobbing made it harder to breathe. "I never should've called her."

My ma stood up and lifted my chin. Her tears had smeared her makeup. "It's not your fault, my love. Accidents happen and that crash was an accident."

My pa sat beside me, placing his hand on my lap. "Don't do this to yourself, son. The only one to blame was that idiot who hit you and Lei." He trembled and balled his fists when he mentioned the drunk driver.

After I had somewhat managed to get myself together, the door of the exam room opened, and Lei was rolled back into the room and to the table. Dr. Iwata logged into the computer and pulled Lei's X-ray up on the monitor. "Your X-rays look good. See these plates and screws?" she asked, pointing to the black and white images on the screen. "They are where they're supposed to be and those—"

"When can I dance again?" Lei interrupted.

"It's going to be a while. You're going to have to wear a cast for another four to six weeks before you can start rehab."

"So when?" Lei pleaded, a heart-wrenching sob making her words difficult to understand.

"Six to ten months."

"No!" Lei screamed. "I'm supposed to go to Juilliard in New York this fall. I worked so hard to get there. Do you know how many girls from Hawai'i get invited to go there?"

"I'm so sorry, Lei," the doctor sympathized.

"I was the first one in almost a decade." Accepting defeat, Lei laid back and stared at the ceiling while tears flowed.

Dr. Iwata and the nurse gave my parents a sympathetic look.

I yanked the door open and ran out of the clinic. I didn't stop running until I found a small garden next to the building. "I'm so sorry, Lei."

* * *

"It wasn't your fault, Kai. It was an accident, like your mother

TWENTY-FIVE: KAI

said," Wyatt told me after I finished telling him what happened the night of the accident and the subsequent events that followed.

"Even though you say that Wyatt, it doesn't change how I feel," I insisted after I wiped tears from my face. "Can we just go home, please," I begged. That was I could handle and I was thankful when Wyatt brought the truck back to life.

"I got us two mochas," I greeted Wyatt when he approached me.

"Is it okay if we stop by Seattle before we head out for our drive?" he asked.

"Of course. Where are we going?"

"I just need to do something. Something I should have done a long time ago."

I held Wyatt's hand tighter and he squeezed back while we walked along the short brick walkway between two patches of green grass. The slate grey colored craftsman's style home trimmed with burgundy window frames that matched the door was surrounded by flower beds with small white daisies on one side and red and yellow variegated dahlias on the other. The white patio was adorned with hanging baskets of violets on all four corners. The wooden swing swayed back and forth from the morning summer breeze.

The door opened and a couple in their fifties looked at us, shocked. The man wearing glasses had a white short-sleeve polo and a pair of khaki pants finished with loafers. But it was the woman who grabbed my attention. Her dark wavy hair was pulled into a neat ponytail. She wore a sleeveless, floral summer dress that flowed to her knees. She clasped both of her hands against her chest and appeared to be crying. She wiped her cheeks before rushing toward us.

Wyatt dropped my hand and met her halfway.

"Wyatt, *Mijo*," she called him, falling into his embrace, and burying her face in his chest.

The man caught up with her and hugged both of them. He removed his glasses to wipe away the tears that had started to fall from his eyes. "My son!" he said.

My vision blurred. The love these three had for each other was oozing from them. I couldn't help but think about my own family. There hadn't been a day that passed where I didn't think of them.

Wyatt turned toward me, his eyes red. "This is Kai. Kai this is Sophia and Carlos Martinez. They're Jim's parents," he introduced everyone.

I extended my hand to shake Sophia's, but to my surprise, she pulled me into a hug.

"It's nice to meet you, Kai." She released me and continued, "Let's get you two inside." She wrapped her arms around us both and guided us toward the open door.

"Can I get you boys anything to drink?" Sophia asked once we were inside.

We sat across from Mr. and Mrs. Martinez in the living room of their home. Pictures of a young man around Wyatt's age, who I assumed was Jim, decorated a section of a brick wall above the fireplace. One picture that stood out was one with Wyatt. They were standing side by side wearing their camo uniform complete with helmets and even with goggles on, I could recognize them. Wyatt had his arms around Jim while Jim gave Wyatt a pair of bunny ears with his fingers. They beamed with pride and joy. It was so nice to see Wyatt free of

TWENTY-FIVE: KAI

the dark cloud that had been haunting him.

Mr. Martinez noticed me studying the picture, so he stood up and took the frame down, and handed it to me. "I love that picture, that smile of his summed-up Jim to a tee. Carefree and so goofy," he chuckled.

Wyatt leaned closer to me to study the picture. "That was our first day in Afghanistan. Everyone was pumped to be there. We had no idea what we were in for." He took a sharp intake of breath before continuing, "I'm sorry I couldn't save him. I promised you I would protect him and I failed." Wyatt dropped his head low and his shoulders sagged.

After placing the frame on the armrest, I placed a hand on his lap while the other rubbed circles on his back.

"That wasn't on you, Son," Mr. Martinez said. "We don't blame you."

Mrs. Martinez rushed toward Wyatt and sat on the coffee table separating the two couches. "You can't do this to yourself, Wyatt. I know why you've avoided our calls. I know why you hid in your house whenever we came to see you," she continued.

Wyatt didn't say anything. He let silent tears fall.

Sophia held Wyatt's chin and lifted his face to meet hers. "We love you, *you are family*. You and Jim were like brothers. We already lost one son in the war, we don't want to lose another. Do you hear me?"

Wyatt nodded, unable to speak.

Twenty-Six: Wyatt

This Reality Was Worse Than Any Nightmare

The sound of beeping machines coupled with the chilliness of the room woke me from a deep sleep. My first attempt to open my eyes failed when a blinding light of yellow and white pierced through my retinas like pins and needles, causing them to shut involuntarily. My eyelids fluttered as I attempted to open them the second time around, slowly giving them time to adjust to the brightness of the room caused by the annoying fluorescent lights above. I found myself lying in a strange bed, with only white linen covering me.

I raised my right arm and followed the thin tube that ran from the top of my hand to the bag of clear solution. Liquid dripped through a small cylindrical chamber which was attached to the bottom of a clear bag and hanging on a thin metal rod. Another set of soft tubes were in my nostrils, hooked to the green oxygen tank over the headboard. 'Military Treatment Hospital' was where I was, according to the words painted on the wall. I was unable to think clearly from being disoriented. But why am I there? *I thought to myself when every part of my body ached, my head was pounding so hard, the pain made me see spots. I finally shut my eyes and let sleep pull me back into oblivion.*

TWENTY-SIX: WYATT

Boom! An explosion rattled Kabul, causing tremors that could be felt for miles. I followed the direction of where our troops fired the grenade launcher, Afghani soldiers were in retreat and running away. My fellow marines scurried down the streets looking for survivors. I leaned forward to pull an injured marine from the street to get them to the convoy, but I wasn't able to grab him. He reached out an arm, and my finger slid once again. Staff Sergeant Bennett grabbed the injured marine's hand and pulled him up to his feet. Cries of agony escaped the injured soldier's mouth when he put pressure on one of his legs. The Staff Sergeant was standing right in front of me, looking in my direction, but not seeing me.

"Where's Martinez?" I asked, but he didn't respond. "Staff Sergeant, have you seen Martinez?" I asked once again, my frustration growing. Stunned, he walked through me as if I were made of air. I was confused. I turned around and followed them, gazing at my hands with concern.

"Wyatt," Martinez's voice took me out of my stupor from what had just happened.

Smoke swirled around a cloud of debris and shadow materialized through the chaos. I recognized Jim, but before I could take a step toward him, a fellow marine pulled Jim up. Jim hung on to the guy as if he were a lifeline on a sinking ship. There was something familiar about the man assisting Jim, even though the guy was covered with black ash and dust like everyone else. From the way he moved to the way he knew how to calm a frantic Jim. Who could that be?

The familiar man put Jim's arm around his shoulder and used his strength to pull them up. He said something to Jim who responded with a nod. The unknown soldier slowly lifted his head just when another plume of rancid smoke wafted around me. I narrowed my eyes to focus on the distorted shadows walking toward me. Their images broke through the billowing blackness that swirled around us and that's when I saw his face.

The man holding Jim was me.

I bored the heels of my palms into my eyes, trying to wipe the image I surely couldn't be seeing. I opened them again, but there I was still holding Jim. My mind reeled. This didn't make any sense. "Jim!" I yelled, but just like Staff Sergeant Bennet, neither he nor the other me acknowledged my call.

"IED," someone yelled from a distance.

My heart raced and I hurried toward them, but before I could even get halfway there, an ear-splitting blast reverberated through me. Burnt fragments and chunks of detritus rained down on the area where the two men were moments before. A few feet away I saw where the other me had landed, but Jim was nowhere to be found. I squinted through the fresh smoke that stung my eyes to assess my wounds. When I patted my torso, I realized that I was unscathed.

The other me moved his arms one by one, then did the same with his legs.

I needed to find Jim and started combing the ground for any signs of him. Spotting Jim's boot through the rising dust and smoke, I rushed to his side. I wasn't ready for the gruesome fact that the leg wasn't attached to a body. Fuck. My stomach twisted in pain but I forced myself to keep looking. The horror gripped me when I took in the charred bits of body parts scattered over the blood-splattered ground. Jim had been blown to pieces and what was left was unrecognizable. My heart stopped and the bloody ground distorted.

I opened my mouth to scream but no sound came out when my soul ripped from my body.

I gasped for air like I had been submerged underwater for a

TWENTY-SIX: WYATT

moment too long and was taking my dying breath when I startled out of my nightmare. Flashes of the ambush and Jim's body played continuously in my mind. Now I understood why I was in the make-shift military hospital.

Soft voices and shadows on the other side of the privacy curtain caught my attention, so I listened closely to their conversation. The hairs on the back of my neck stood up when I realized that they weren't speaking English. No, they were speaking Arabic. Those motherfuckers were here to kill me.

I closed my eyes and relaxed my body, pretending to be asleep when their voices got closer. I counted to three before I opened my eyes, and lunged toward the man at the side of my bed. My suspicions had been right, he was one of the Afghani soldiers. I grabbed him by the throat, my force dropping us to the floor. I applied more pressure as I straddle him from above to incapacitate the man sent to finish me off. "I'm going to fucking kill you," I barked as I put more pressure on the kill.

* * *

"Wyatt," a breathy voice called.

Ignoring it, I continued to put more pressure on the enemy's neck. I was going to break it, but I wanted to see him suffer first and look into the eyes of death before he took his last breath. I wouldn't give him mercy, not for what he did to Jim.

"Wyatt, it's me," the voice called once again, a hand caressing my face. "It's me, Kai."

I blinked in confusion at the mention of Kai's name. I looked around the room expecting to see a hospital bed in the military hospital. Instead, I was in a dark bedroom.

A muffled moan caused me to look down and I saw Kai pinned beneath me with my hands wrapped around his neck.

It's just a dream, it's just a dream, it's just a dream.

Horror and shame hurdled me into a cruel reality. This was worse than any nightmare.

I released him from my hold so swiftly that it caused me to tumble to the floor and knocked the wind out of me.

"Wyatt," Kai gasped before his shocked face appeared over the side of the bed. "Are you okay?"

I shook my head and looked at my shaking hands. Did I really just choke Kai?

Kai rubbing the red marks on his neck made my stomach curdle. "Wyatt?"

I averted my eyes. What if I hadn't woken up? What if I had succeeded? My heart skipped before attempting to pound through my ribs. I covered my face to hide.

"Wyatt? Look at me please?" Kai begged after my extended silence. His voice was breaking. The covers rustled when he climbed off the bed. His fingers caressed my hands before he pried them open so he could look into my eyes. "I'm okay, see?"

I shook my head, afraid to utter a sound. My fear of becoming that guy was coming true.

"Please let me in," Kai pleaded. When I didn't respond, he continued, "Why won't you let me in?"

I couldn't tell him. He'd never understand, no one ever did. I've been alone for so long, I never thought I needed someone until that evening when he saw me crumbling. He wiped away my tears tenderly with his thumbs. I didn't know I was crying. I wanted to have him, and I wanted to be his, but I was broken and dangerous.

"Talk to me," he urged.

Too exhausted to fight, I took a deep breath and spoke, "Darkness is all I know, Kai, and the light you bring threatens to expose all the cuts and scars I hide. I don't want you to wake up one day and only see the broken pieces of me."

Twenty-Seven: Kai

Please Don't Go

Was I afraid for my life? *Yes,* but I also knew that the man who had his hands wrapped around my neck wasn't my Wyatt. The man I knew wouldn't lay a finger on me. He was someone who made me smile, made me happy. So, as much as a part of me wanted to flee in the same way I did when my manipulative and abusive ex hit me, a part of me needed to stay with Wyatt and fight this battle with him.

"I'm so fucking sorry, Kai, I'm so sorry," Wyatt had found his voice while he grabbed his underwear from the floor sliding into them in a hurry, followed by his pants. The horror that had been there when he realized what he'd done was still reflecting in his haunted eyes. He was shutting down once again.

"Wyatt, talk to me please?"

"I need to go. This is a mistake. This whole thing with you and I was a mistake," his voice was breaking, trying to stop from crying.

My chest tightened. "Don't say that."

"I never should've let it get this far," he rambled after pulling his shirt on. His eyes captured mine and the dark grey storm threatened to break me. "I'm sorry Kai," he continued. "I can't

TWENTY-SEVEN: KAI

do this anymore."

My attempt to touch him was met with a hand in the air, telling me to back off. Wyatt was gone, he'd shut down again and the man standing in front of me was someone I didn't recognize. The cold gesture made me step back with an uncontrollable whimper. I was still skittish after my experience with Noah. But I wasn't willing to give up on Wyatt yet.

I moved to stand in front of the bedroom door to prevent him from leaving me. It was a pathetic attempt to make him stay because he could plow through me in his sleep, but I trusted that he had no intentions of hurting me. "I love you, Wyatt. Remember when you asked me why I came here?" I asked him, trying to reopen the connection between us. "I came to San Juan looking for a fresh start and I found it with you," I continued, wiping my tears with the back of my hand. "Please stay and talk to me?"

Wyatt shook his head. "I'm not the fresh start you're looking for. I'm no one's *fresh start*. I'm everyone's bitter ending." His shoulders dropped and he looked away. Then he tensed again as if was gearing up for a fight. "You don't get it, Kai. What happened just now is something that's never happened before." He turned his back to me and ran a hand over his face, while the other rested on his waist. "I'm not getting any better, I'm getting worse. My whole life sucks. It always will."

"Life sucks for everyone, Wyatt, not just yours. And it'll always try to knock us down any chance it gets. But we can't wait for it to be perfect to allow ourselves to love again, to be happy. Why do you shut people out?" I asked his back.

"That's fucking rich coming from you, the same person who ran away from home and ignores his family's calls every day."

A dry laugh followed the venom that came out of his mouth. He was right, I was no better. "Hit a nerve, Kai? That's what I thought."

I knew that I'd lost the battle. He was right. I was a hypocrite and I needed to hear it.

Wyatt turned around when I didn't answer his question. I could feel his eyes on me when I walked past him to the bed. I couldn't meet his scathing gaze. I climbed into bed and stared at the window so I didn't have to watch him leave.

I felt like I was floating on a tidal wave out to sea in the middle of a tropical storm. The door slammed so hard it made the windows rattle in protest.

Wyatt was gone.

I was a fool for trying to save him. He might be broken, but he made me realize how damaged I was too. I stared unseeing at the wall for hours. My phone screen lit up and I saw that my parents were calling me like they did every single morning. For the first time since I left Oahu, I accepted the call.

"Kai?" I could hear the surprise in Ma's voice.

Choking on the words, my voice sounded alien to me. "Ma? I'm coming home."

Sam opened the door after a couple of knocks and I felt guilty for interrupting her evening with my impromptu visit, but I had two hours to make my flight back to Hawai'i. "I'm sorry to drop in unannounced, but will you please drop this off at The San Juan Winds office and give it to Wyatt?"

"Of course, do you have time to come in?" she asked. I'd given her the news yesterday that I wasn't going to extend my lease and offered to leave the bed and sofa. She'd expressed

TWENTY-SEVEN: KAI

her disappointment in seeing me go and tried to convince me to stay, but I needed to face my demons so I could start healing and become a better person.

"I can't. The airport shuttle is waiting for me. I just wanted to ask this one last favor," I explained after she accepted the container.

She pulled me into a hug. "I'm sorry to see you go, Kai," she said.

A flood of emotion hit me and I tried to push it away as I hugged her back. "Me, too. Thank you for everything, Sam. Text me if you're ever in Hawai'i," I whispered. I stepped back because my chest was hurting. "Later, Sam," I said because I hoped to see her again.

With a heavy heart, I forced my legs to carry me to the shuttle that was waiting at the curb. I was once again saying goodbye to an island that had become my home.

"Are you ready?" the driver asked once I climbed into the backseat.

I stared at my phone, my thumb hovering above Wyatt's name. I tapped his name and listened to it ring twice before it went to voicemail. Swallowing around the lump in my throat, I tried to ignore the crack in my voice, "Yes."

Twenty-Eight: Wyatt

He's Gone

I took my fifth Tylenol of the day to relieve the splitting headache I'd suffered the past three days since I walked out on Kai. He'd tried to call me, and he even stopped by my house and camped out on my porch several times, but I didn't answer because there was nothing else left to say. I was afraid to hurt him both physically and emotionally. I was kidding myself when I believed I could live a normal life. I could never be normal and Kai was only a fantasy.

"What's happening, buddy," Avery finally broke the tense silence that had been lingering since I got there. He walked to the front of my desk and drummed his fingers on the hard surface. I didn't give them the reason why I didn't show up to work for two days. Thankfully, they knew me well enough to know not to push. But Avery must have had enough. "You can't just keep going MIA for days at a time like this. Where were you?" he scolded.

I didn't have time for his shit. Why can't he just let me be? Ignoring his question and his existence altogether, I placed my elbows on my desk and massaged my temples with my sight focused on the spreadsheets in front of me. I had disappointed

TWENTY-EIGHT: WYATT

everyone. I couldn't even look at the innocent face of Elijah beaming at me from the framed picture on my desk without feeling like a rusty, dull blade had carved out my heart.

I was a danger to everybody.

Avery started rapping the desk impatiently with his knuckles. "Wyatt? What happened to us being a team? We run this business together, you know?" he asked with a firm voice.

I swear it felt like someone was driving an ice pick into my head with each rap of his knuckles. "I'm sorry you had to sail for me, okay? I didn't mean to interrupt your perfect little life," I barked. I wanted to fight him to let my frustration, shame, and guilt which had been building, erupt.

Avery stopped rapping his knuckles and his eyes narrowed. "I don't fucking care about sailing or work, you fucker. We care about you," he said with emotion I didn't expect when he gestured to Elizabeth. "Did you even think about that? And why was Kai looking for you? Why haven't you been answering his calls... or our calls for that matter?" he asked fuming.

"Sweetie, just leave him alone," Elizabeth said, trying to calm him down.

"No babe, I've let him do this to himself for too long. This ends today," he explained to her before turning his attention back to me. "You can hate me, Wyatt, but we're going to help you through this whether you want our help or not."

That was what I needed to hear. The wall that I had shoved every horrific emotion behind began to crumble. I sobbed into my hands when the agony drowned me.

Elizabeth rushed to bolt the door and flipped the open sign to *closed.*

Avery kicked my chair away from the desk and pulled me

into his arms before I knew what was happening. "We've got you, brother," his gruff voice whispered.

Elizabeth wrapped her arms around both of us. "We love you so much, Wyatt."

Needing to unload some of my torment, I wiped some of my tears on Avery's shoulder before I said, "I hurt him. He's never going to forgive me for what I said, for what I did." I separated myself from their embrace and flopped into my chair. Staring on the scuffed floor, I told them about the nightmare and how I hurt Kai.

Avery gripped my shoulder when he heard about the choking. "Fuck, Wyatt. He—"

A knock on the door surprised us and a woman waved to get our attention. I recognized her as Sam Matthews, Kai's landlord. I wiped my face, ashamed she might see my tears.

Elizabeth rushed to open the door. "We're closed right now. You can check our website to book a tour."

Sam lifted a document tube. "I have something for Wyatt. From Kai," she explained.

I stood up at the mention of Kai's name and I was at the door in a heartbeat. "Come in," I urged. *What if something happened to him? He stopped calling and texting last night.* "What about Kai? Is he okay?" I asked Sam, my voice shaking with fear.

Seeing the panic in my eyes, Sam hesitated. "He stopped by last night and asked me to give you this." She handed me the tube which I opened immediately. It contained a blueprint that was labeled *The San Juan Winds* at the top. There was a small yellow post-it attached to it that read:

I hope this plan works. Take care of yourself. - Kai

"Where's Kai?" Elizabeth asked Sam.

"He's gone," she said.

TWENTY-EIGHT: WYATT

"What do you mean gone? Did he tell you where he was going?" I asked, my chest tightening while I kept the emotions from coming out once again.

"Home. He asked me to drop this off since you haven't been answering his calls. Sorry, Wyatt," Sam said with a frown. "I'm sorry to interrupt, but this felt important. I hope your night gets better," she said before heading out.

I stared at the door, not really seeing it. "He's gone, just like everyone else."

"Wait a minute," Avery started.

"Wyatt?" Elizabeth called.

Their voices sounded static. "Fuck him, I don't need him." I grabbed my keys off the desk and walked out, ignoring my friends' pleas for me to stay.

He left.

I was alone again and that was fine. I would be fine. I wouldn't miss the way he said my name like it was a prayer. I wouldn't miss how his touch made me feel cherished and alive. I wouldn't miss the way he laughed or his laugh brought a smile to everyone's face. I wouldn't miss his smile that made everything alright.

I was fine.

I wouldn't miss his stupid rankings about shit.

This was how it was always going to end. I was just kidding myself thinking that maybe, just maybe I could have him. Afraid I was going to be broken for the rest of my life, I unlocked my phone and searched for the only person who might be able to help me. "I need to see you tomorrow. It's an emergency."

Chapter Twenty-Nine: Kai

Home Again, Only I Wasn't

A knock on the door jarred me awake. I rolled over and remembered I was in my old bedroom in my ohana's home. It was late in the evening when Pa picked me up from the airport. After what happened between Wyatt and me, I booked the first available flight out of Seattle. I was back home in Hawai'i, only it didn't feel like home.

Another knock rattled my door.

"Kai, are you up?" Lei called after a brief silence.

"Come in, Lei."

The door opened and Lei came in. She was no longer walking with her crutches, but I couldn't miss the pronounced limp when she walked toward me.

I tore my gaze from her and focused on the polished cement floor instead. I sat up and twisted out of the covers, hanging my feet off the bed, when Lei sat beside me.

"It's getting better," she said while she extended her leg up.

"Lei, I'm so—"

"Stop it, Kuya," she interrupted my apology and turned to face me. "Stop saying you're sorry. It's not your fault. What can we say to make you believe us? You know what you should

CHAPTER TWENTY-NINE: KAI

be sorry for?" she asked.

Clueless, I just looked into eyes that almost matched mine and shook my head.

"You should be sorry for walking away. For ignoring our calls. For making us feel like we don't matter. Because that hurt more than anything."

I reached out to wipe the tears that were flowing down her cheeks then wrapped my arms around her. "I'm sorry for all of that," I whispered through her hair. "I'm here now, and I will never leave our ohana again."

Another knock from the door grabbed both our attention and we pulled away from each other's embrace. "Come in," I called out and Mikaela came in.

"Ma said you're back. Nice to see ya." Mikaela rushed toward me and gave me a kiss on the cheek and a hug.

"It's so nice to see you," I said, matching her enthusiasm.

"I knew you wouldn't last that long being away from Hawai'i," she teased.

My smile faltered at that comment.

Mikaela frowned and looked at Lei who gave her a shrug. "What's wrong?"

"Nothing." I swallowed the sadness that was threatening to envelop me. The sadness had possessed me since I left Seattle for good. I shouldn't feel this way. They said red was the color of love, but why am I so blue? Not even the presence of my family could tear me out of this gloom. I missed Wyatt, it's only been a few days since I saw him last, but my heartfelt hollow. I tried to keep fighting for us, but that battle was too massive for one person to soldier on.

"Are you okay, Kuya?" Lei rubbed my back and I found both of them staring at me when I looked up.

"Yeah, just jet lag is all. I'll be fine."

"Okay, I'm gonna be late for work. I'll see you at dinner tonight, ya?" Mikaela said. She left the room and waved goodbye.

"I heard from Julliard," Lei said once Mikaela had gone.

I held my breath and the all-consuming guilt tried to surface until Lei continued.

"They are extending their invitation until next year when I'm all healed." Her eyes became glossy with tears.

I hugged her and blew out a breath. "That's great. I am so happy for you. No one deserves it more than you do. You worked so hard and you're amazing."

"Thank you, now please do us all a favor. Let go of the guilt. We want our Kai back."

"I'm supposed to be the mature one here, and yet here you're giving life lessons. Jesus! You're too wise for your own good. You know that?" I teased.

As expected, Ma and Pa had thrown a luau celebrating my homecoming. They'd find any excuse to have a party. Everyone was gathered on the spacious lanai, lined up to sample Ma's famous recipes. The temperature was perfect for an outdoor gathering. You could smell the plumeria blooms from Ma's favorite tree by the fence that separated us from the road.

Even with everyone around, someone was missing, and that someone was twenty-five hundred miles away. I was missing him so much, but I wanted to be present at my gathering and with my ohana.

I sneaked inside the house to have a moment to myself.

"What's wrong, Kai? Are you still tired from the trip?" Ma

CHAPTER TWENTY-NINE: KAI

asked, interrupting my thoughts of Wyatt.

I shook my head as tears cascaded down my cheeks. Ma led me to my bedroom and once we were inside, I let everything out. The valve that was holding all the pressure from the accident, the San Juan Islands and Wyatt, was about to burst open. I told her everything and she listened.

"I'm sorry about that, Kai. We're always here for you. We will support you in whatever you want to do. I just want you to be happy. That is what all parents want. This Wyatt sounds like a great guy, but this is his journey. Only he can determine his final destination. Do you understand what I'm saying?"

"I do, Ma."

"We love you, Kai."

"I love you too, Ma. Let's enjoy the party outside.".

Thirty: Wyatt

Humor me

"Humor me, Wyatt," Dr. Tina A. McAndrew broke the silence minutes after I'd arrived in her office at Seattle's VA Hospital. She leaned back in her plush chair, supporting her elbow on the armrest, her chin resting on her knuckles while she studied me. Her wavy shoulder-length hair framed her angelic face. She wasn't wearing a lot of makeup, but her red lips stood out from her brown skin. It was hard to tell how old she was, but if the dates on her certificates were any indication, she had to be in her early forties.

To avoid her questioning eyes, I studied the diploma directly to her right. The words *Uniformed Services University* stared right back at me. Dr. McAndrew cleared her throat before she continued, "You've been coming here every month for four years without fail, but you never talk." She narrowed her eyes while studying me, perhaps trying to get a reaction out of me. "Why do you keep showing up?" she asked while crossing her arms. She paused for a while and I thought she was done talking about this nonsense.

I started shifting in my seat, unsure where this one-way conversation was going. With her stare making me uneasy,

THIRTY: WYATT

I couldn't hold her gaze for more than a second fearing she could see that it had affected me. My eyes traveled around the nondescript room, avoiding her eye contact.

"I know why you're here," she began again, much to my chagrin.

I shook my head and huffed out a breath about the absurdity of her statement, and immediately cursed myself for showing any emotion.

"And not because of what's on your file. I know why you're here at nine o'clock in the morning every first Monday of every month without fail. So, Wyatt, do you want to tell me why, or should I tell you?"

I met her stare, giving her daggers of my own. Who the hell did she think she was talking to me like I was some kind of idiot? She didn't fucking know anything. My hands were getting clammy and even with the windows open, I felt like I couldn't breathe. *Thirty minutes more. Thirty minutes more.* I'd be out of here in thirty minutes. All I had to do was sit through this bullshit.

"The VA is the only place that makes you feel like a soldier, *Lance Corporal Miller*, because out there, outside the halls of this hospital, you're just Wyatt."

I balled my hand into a fist, fumes coming out of my nose. My heavy breathing stressed the tension in the room. I closed my eyes to collect myself. *I will not let her win.*

"Being just Wyatt is good. You deserve to be just Wyatt after what you've done for this country."

Another silence.

"Does the truth make you uncomfortable, Wyatt?"

I'm uncomfortable every day, from the moment I wake up until I go to bed. The only time I seemed to get a reprieve was when I was with Kai. I didn't tell her that, it would only give her more ammunition.

"So that's one of the reasons why you're here every month. Do you want to tell me the other one?"

I swallowed hard, giving away my poker face. I glanced at my watch. *Twenty-five more minutes.*

"Or should I tell you that too?" she continued, unaffected.

I stood up, having had enough of that interrogation. "You don't know shit about me. I'm not some kind of experiment that you could base your theories on," I finally said pointing a finger at her.

If Dr. McAndrew was shocked by my outburst, she didn't show it. She didn't even flinch. She leaned back in her chair, placing both of her hands on each armrest again.

"You don't get to mock me. I know I'm not a soldier anymore." Exhausted, I sat back in the chair with my head down, "Every day is a reminder of that." I thought about the hundreds of times I felt worthless because all I did was exist. "I was finally okay just being me for once," I whispered, surprised that I'd said it out loud. I didn't mean to, but that was the truth.

"Why was that Wyatt," Dr. McAndrew asked, her voice laced with sympathy this time. "What changed since the last time you were here?"

I lifted my head and met her eyes, the notepad that was in her lap moved to the table by her side, and she was patiently waiting for a response. "When I'm with Kai, I'm just Wyatt, not the shattered hero everyone felt sorry for."

Her eyes softened for a split second before schooling her expression to the neutral look I'd come to know. She let a few seconds pass before grabbing her pen and notepad back and continuing with our session. "Where is Kai now?"

THIRTY: WYATT

I'd seen that question coming and even if I had been expecting it, I still felt clueless about how to answer. He probably didn't want to ever see me again, especially after what I'd done and said to him a couple of days ago. I missed him, the way he uprooted my life in a matter of weeks was scary, and just like in the past, I chose the easy way out. To hide and shield me from anything, in this case, anyone, who could hurt me. Denial had worked before, it will again.

"Have you reached out to Kai?"

"It doesn't matter, Nothing happened and calling him will not change anything," I said while avoiding her probing stare once again.

"Nothing happened?" Dr. McAndrew crossed her arms as she leaned back before continuing, "So you're telling me, that you called my cell phone last night, using the number I gave you for emergency use only, and insisted to meet me today, a week before your appointment because my couch is comfy?"

The tension in the room was palpable, heightened by the humming of the ceiling fan. I'd hoped she'd buy my initial excuse and just fix me. The other reason why I come here every month. I want her to just *fix me*.

"I told him that he shouldn't be with me. I told him that those episodes he'd witnessed would never go away. I told him that he's better off with someone else, and to forget he ever knew me." My chest tightened hearing those words all over again. He'd shown me nothing but love and kindness, and what did I do in return? Hurt him. "I told him that I don't want to see him again. So he left. He's gone." The sob that ripped from me was unfamiliar and if it wasn't for the fact that there were only two of us in the room, I could have sworn it was coming from someone else.

"Wyatt, it was Kai's choice to be with you. Only he can decide how to live his life, and to whom he'd want to share his with."

"I hurt him. It's better this way, before whatever it was between him and I goes too far." Something was telling me it was already too late, that the hole in my heart would be the cross I'd bear for the rest of my life.

"What's the other reason you're here?"

Moment of truth. I'd told her more than I'd ever told anyone. More than Avery and Elizabeth, more than my support group leader, even more than Kai. The next few words should be easy, but the words refused to come out. I opened my mouth, but nothing.

Another deep breath.

"I want you to fix me, I need you to make this go away. I'm so damned tired of being afraid, being broken. I just want to be normal, so fix me… please?"

Sniffing caught my attention and when I looked up, Dr. McAndrew wiped the steady stream of tears from her cheeks. She sighed deeply before, she continued, "I wish there was a pill I could give you to free you from all of this. We can't change what happened in the past, it will always be there no matter how hard we try to suppress it. What you have the power to change, is your future. What do you want your future to look like Lance Corporal?"

Hell, if I know. One thing I knew for sure, I needed to soldier on.

I was sitting in the same parking lot in front of a nondescript beige building waiting for the clock to strike eight o'clock the day after my session with Dr. McAndrew. I'd been there many

THIRTY: WYATT

times before, but unlike those times, I wanted to be there. The urge to run away was nowhere to be found and all I could hear was Dr. McAndrew's questions when I saw her. *"What do you want your future to look like Lance Corporal?"* I didn't know, but I knew who I wanted to be with.

I was tired of hiding.

Just like clockwork, car doors began opening and out of them came the familiar faces of my group. I didn't know their names, but I remembered their stories. I used to wonder why they had to keep coming and sharing the same stories over and over again, but I finally understood the reason.

Coming here gave them hope.

It took years for me to realize that, but it was hope that better days were ahead. Hope that someday the pain would hurt less, and hope that someday I would be worthy enough for Kai.

I hoped it wasn't too late.

"It took a lot for me to come here and share my story," I said before the leader was able to gather everyone to start the session. Some people were settling down, some were still standing behind their seats or had just entered the room. But no one asked me to stop talking, so I kept going. "Not because I didn't want to or I didn't try." They all stopped and looked at me with compassion. I felt vulnerable and exposed, I closed my eyes and swallowed my anxiety. I feared that looking at them would make me want to run, but the look of understanding and the slight nods from the group encouraging me to keep going, greeted me as soon as I opened my eyes. "You see, I'm not only hurting physically but I'm hurting emotionally too," I blinked away my tears. I didn't care if they thought of me as weak. "The war took more than just my friends," I continued. I ran my hand to my chest where the dog tag of my fallen brother hung. A gesture formed out of habit whenever I think about him. "It took away my light and now, all I can see is darkness."

"I struggle every day, but I keep going, believing that my life will somehow get better. That I could get better. Some say I'm a fighter," a humorless laugh escaped my mouth, and I shook my head. "But I know I'm not."

"Making decisions was easier when it was just me that I had to worry about. It's a lot tougher when you have to consider another person as well. Especially when that person is someone very important to you." An image of Kai appeared in my head and it made me want to run and hide from my shame. "The thing is, I started feeling better. I finally met someone who made me want to try harder, but I hurt him."

"I can't afford to go into that hole anymore. Just getting by is no longer an acceptable option for me. I have to do more than just existing. I have to start living. The kind of living I did when I was with him. The last few weeks had been the best time of my life." I lifted my head, to see heads nodding with understanding. I looked at Jason, our support group leader and he stood up and walked toward me.

He placed his hand on my shoulder, followed by a squeeze. "I'm proud of you Wyatt, we all are. Everyone here knows how hard it is to do what you just did." He looked around as everyone nodded in agreement with his statement. "Bravery comes in different forms and what you just did, that was very brave." He began clapping, slow at first, then faster and the whole group followed.

Taking turns, fellow soldiers came up to me to show their support. "I'm so proud of you Wyatt," a man who I knew lost his wife last year told me.

THIRTY: WYATT

"Thank you for sharing your story," a woman said. Her son was missing in combat.

"It's going to get better. The horrors we experienced are always going to be there," another man said, and touched my chest where my heart was, "but with time, you'll find the good in life again. You'll see, I promise it gets better," he continued.

I hadn't won this battle, but for the first time since I started coming here and going to see Dr. McAndrew, I was looking forward to the prospect of tomorrow. I didn't want to do this alone, not anymore.

Thirty-One: Kai

Heart Wants What It Wants

E verything was the same but felt so different, even when I was surrounded by waves. Waves had always been my sanctuary where I felt the most alive, but my heart now belonged somewhere else. With someone else, and he had no idea. It had been about a week since I left the San Juan Islands and had seen him. I loved him and I knew he loved me too, but the flame our love ignited wasn't enough to thaw the wall frozen around Wyatt's heart. I wasn't enough to fuel his desire to fight for us. I tried, but in the end, we just burned out.

I wasn't strong enough to fight for both of us. A small part of me echoed that this was how it was always supposed to end, but I didn't want to believe it. I wanted our story to have a different ending.

Maybe it was for the best.

"Have you tried calling him?" Mikaela asked. She was floating next to me, sitting on her board with her legs dangling over both sides like me. We'd let prime waves go by and I felt bad for dragging her out just to sit in silence.

I caught her up on everything about San Juan, including

THIRTY-ONE: KAI

the horrible evening I had with Wyatt. Knowing how protective she was, I thought she'd be the last person who would encourage me to call him. I shook my head *no*.

"Do you think he meant what he said to you?" she continued.

"It doesn't matter. It's over. I've been there before."

"I have a feeling this is different, Kai. You should call him."

"I called him for days!" I said with annoyance. "I called him, I sat outside his door for hours begging him to talk to me. I even went by his work. It's over."

"Ya sure?" she asked, appraising me as she splashed ocean water on her arms to cool off.

"I'm gonna take a break from this chat," I said to Mikaela needing to move on. "You should join them." I hooked a thumb where some of our friends were riding the surf.

"Okay, join us in a bit, ya?"

All I managed to do was nod and watch as Mikaela lay face down on her board, and started paddling with her hands in the direction of the group.

Instead of joining the group, I paddled to the beach and dropped my board on the sand. It landed face down which wasn't great since I'd just waxed it earlier that morning, but I didn't have the energy to care. I flopped next to it and watched my friends enjoy the waves, and wondered what Wyatt was doing. I looked down and dug my feet into the sand and closed my eyes, pretending that I was sitting on a beach twenty-five hundred miles northeast instead. Where the water was frigid and the air was cool.

"Surfers are like nine out of ten when it comes to the scale of hotness."

My head jolted up, and every nerve cell fired, reviving every fiber of my being. I stayed still, hoping that I wasn't hallucinating his voice. The sand behind me began to shift as footsteps came closer. I inhaled deeply when I caught a whiff of a familiar clean scent carried by leeward winds. The scent that was forever tattooed into my memory, and will forever be associated with joy and love.

"Wyatt," I whispered.

He sat next to me and continued, "You're right. This beach is beautiful, better than I imagined."

A stray tear fell from my eye and onto the sand because I was overwhelmed by his presence. I turned to face him. I didn't realize how much I'd missed him until I looked into his eyes. He looked so out of place in a pair of jeans and a blue long-sleeve shirt that was rolled up to his elbows and soaked with sweat.

"Aloha Joe was out of everything, but chips. Imagine my disappointment after flying over five hours and finding out that lunch would be Doritos," he continued as he stared into my eyes.

"Nine out of ten, huh?" I asked when I finally recovered from the shock. I wanted to jump all over him, but I was hesitant after everything that had happened.

He cupped my face and I felt like a magnet pulled us together. His lips were frantic against mine in a kiss so passionate, it was like he needed oxygen and I was his air. "A surfer in my arms is the hottest," he answered with his forehead leaning against mine.

"Any surfers?" I teased.

"No, just you, Kai Lobo. Only you. I'm so sorry for what I did, for the horrible things I said. You have to know that I didn't mean any of it. I'd never want to intentionally hurt you and I'm—"

THIRTY-ONE: KAI

I didn't let him continue. "I know you'd never hurt me, Wyatt." I knew he was sorry for choking me and he only said those things so I would walk away. "But that's not what I want to hear from you."

"I love you, and I will do everything I can to be the man you deserve."

"There's only one way this could work, Wyatt, and this is not negotiable if you want to be with me. Don't shut me out ever again. I can deal with the attacks and the gloom, but I need to know that you'll never turn your back on me again. I want to be strong for us, and that comes with the security that I can also lean on you. I will be there as much or as little as you want. But I will always be there for you."

He nodded and lunged toward me, causing me to lay back on the sand. He caged my head between his two hands, looking at me as if we were the only ones on the beach. "I love you so much, I've never felt like this with anyone. I'm home when I'm with you. You make me want to be better. I'm sorry I let you doubt my feelings for you." He slowly lowered his head to kiss me.

"You must be Wyatt?" Mikaela asked before dropping her board next to mine.

"Yes," Wyatt answered, looking back and forth between us. He pushed to a stand and reached out a hand to pull me up. "Are you Mikaela?" he guessed.

"Da one and only," she answered before hugging Wyatt, catching him off guard. "Perfect timing, Ma just texted me." She showed her Apple Watch to me showing me Ma's message, *'lunch is ready'.*

"Want to meet my ohana?" I asked Wyatt hesitantly.

He surprised me by saying, "I'd love to." He reached out to

hold my hand.

Mikaela must have given them the news of Wyatt's arrival since everyone was waiting for us by the door.

"I'm going to apologize in advance," I said looking at Wyatt apologetically. "You think I'm too much? Be prepared for a whole dose of Lobo's."

"Kai, it's okay. I'd love to meet your family." He brought my hand to his lips in front of everyone to see and he took the lead dragging me with him. "My name is Wyatt—" he wasn't able to finish his introduction because my ma threw herself at him for a hug.

"Aloha to Hawai'i, Wyatt," my pa shook his hand awkwardly since Ma hadn't released him from her embrace.

Lei approached to give me a side hug. I was thankful once again that she was no longer using her crutches since her recovery had been better than expected.

"You must be, Lei," Wyatt said when Ma finally released him.

"I am," she responded.

"It's nice to meet you, Lei," Wyatt said after Lei hugged him.

"Let's all go inside, lunch is ready," Ma called.

"What's the occasion?" Wyatt asked once we were seated at the table in front of an assortment of local food. I could see why he would think that we were about to have a celebration. Ma didn't know how to cook small batches of food and our culture valued cooking and eating so much that it was always a luau. Dishes were piled up with heaps of Kalua Pork, Chicken Adobo, Poi, Kimchi Fried Rice, and Haupia.

"Nothing, we just love to eat," I chuckled.

"Wyatt, try this," Ma said and handed him the plate of Kalua Pork.

"This one is good too," Pa said, putting a heaping spoonful

of Kimchi Fried Rice on his plate.

"Thank you," he said with his eyes darting between my parents who were loading up his plate with a bit of everything.

"Where are ya staying?" Mikaela asked.

Wyatt looked at me before answering, "I came in such a hurry, I haven't booked anything yet."

"Don't book anything, stay here," Ma insisted.

"You've been gracious enough, I can stay downtown," Wyatt said.

"We insist," she said and reached over the table to hold Pa's hand.

Wyatt looked at me for approval so I answered for him. "He'd love to stay here."

Thirty-Two: Wyatt

You're Mine and I'm Yours

"Are you sure it's not a problem?" I asked, looking around Kai's small, childhood bedroom while I sat on his bed.

"In our culture, the more the merrier and you're always welcome in my family home. Trust me, my family is happy to have you here."

An awkward silence lingered between Kai and me. The tension was once again back, and I only had myself to blame. Coming here wasn't enough, I needed to convince Kai that I was dedicated to making this work, and I was willing to do anything to win him back. He stood by the doorway, biting his fingernails. It was a side of him that I wasn't used to.

"Can I hold you, Kai?" I asked hesitantly.

Instead of answering, Kai walked toward me and I parted my legs so he could stand between them. He wrapped his arms around my neck, his hands playing with my hair.

I leaned my forehead against his chest.

I felt a kiss on top of my head and Kai lifted my chin to meet his eyes that were filled with so many questions.

I cleared my throat and took a deep breath, digging deep

inside me to find the courage I needed to tell this man how much I needed him. I started with my visit with Dr. McAndrew and ended with my session with the support group.

"I'm so proud of you, Wyatt," he said, his gaze never leaving mine.

"It's a long time coming. The thought of not seeing you again, not being able to touch you again, wasn't the future I wanted. It's going to take a lot of work since I wasted four years," I explained.

"You didn't waste them. You needed that time," he assured me before pressing a soft kiss to my lips.

His bedroom was small but at least he had his own bathroom. I wondered if being invited to stay also meant being invited to sleep in his room.

"I'm going to take a quick shower, make yourself comfortable," Kai announced when he pulled out of our embrace.

I was nervous and unsure of where exactly our relationship stood, and whether we would be able to pick up where we left off. I heard the shower turn on and the sliding of a shower curtain opening. I could visualize Kai slipping naked into it and I had a strong urge to join him. But I was reluctant. I didn't usually have issues with control and making decisions about my life, but being here with Kai made me a bundle of nerves. I kicked my shoes off and laid back on the bed, fighting my desire to go join him.

The water turned off and I heard him once again stepping around the curtain. The door was open, so it would have been easy to just step in, but I wanted to give him space. My visit was certainly a surprise, and I didn't want to overstep.

"You want to shower?" he asked, stepping back into the room with a towel wrapped around his waist. His skin was darker with a hint of redness, no doubt from him being back in his beloved Hawaiian sun.

"Yes, that'd be great."

"More towels are in the cabinet by the sink, help yourself."

Kai opened a dresser drawer and pulled out a pair of briefs. He turned his back to me and dropped the towel, standing there naked before he pulled them on. The sight of his perfect ass had my mind quickly going back to every single time I'd been with him and how much I loved his body. I loved feeling it and being in it. The overwhelming desire to pick him up and throw him onto the bed had me weak-kneed. I needed this man. I wanted to make love to him.

I grabbed my duffel bag and walked into the bathroom. I hadn't undressed in the other room because I had a raging hard-on. Even though I wanted to bury myself in Kai, I also desired the emotional connection between us too.

I quickly showered and returned to the darkened room. A small night light was next to his nightstand dimly illuminating the room, and the ceiling fan made soft whispers. Because of the warm night, Kai was laying on top of the sheets.

I knew he wasn't asleep even though his eyes were closed. He wasn't resting naturally, and I could sense he was as nervous as I was. Our arms were inches apart, and my skin was burning with desire because I needed to touch him. I moved my hand across the top sheet and brought it to rest next to his hip. He jumped slightly but made no attempt to move away. I was well aware that we both needed to break the silence, break through the fear and reconnect. Kai moved a tiny bit closer, our shoulders touched, and I felt the warmth of his skin. There was a faint hint of a coconut fragrance coming from him and I assumed it was lotion to help with his mild sunburn. He

THIRTY-TWO: WYATT

smelled incredible and I wanted to inhale every inch of him.

I moved my eyes down to his crotch and noticed that he was fully erect through his briefs, obviously craving to touch and release as much as I was.

I lifted my hand up and along his hip moving across his flat stomach, brushing gently across the tip of his cock, that was already straining against sexy underwear. It sprang to attention from the simple touch I'd made, so I laid my hand directly on his length, feeling its hardness. Kai flexed several times and I felt his cock swelling. Encouraged, I slid down the bed and in between his legs, moving them apart. I moved his briefs to the side to free his cock and slowly licked from his balls all the way to the tip eliciting a moan from Kai. I was disappointed that he kept his hands stiffly at his sides, but he wasn't halting my advances so I figured I had the green light to proceed. I reached for his cock and pulled it away from his body and wrapped my lips around the engorged head, swirling my tongue before slurping the entire length into my mouth. I held his cock in my mouth when he lifted his hips off the bed, meeting me eagerly.

I continued to suck on his dick and massage his balls as his hips thrust into me. My hands went up and down his shaft, moist saliva lubricating him.

"That feels amazing Wyatt, I've missed this so much," he whispered, moving his hands to the sides of my head, guiding me back and forth over his erection.

"You're so fucking beautiful, I couldn't stand waiting a moment longer," I responded, holding his cock with my hands before swallowing it deep again. I pulled his underwear down and away from his body, tossing them to the floor.

Kai continued to rhythmically fuck my mouth with his cock,

his hands firmly holding my head and controlling the pace. I noticed him slightly lift his legs, bending at the knee, a natural move to remind me he had a beautiful ass, and it was wanting some attention too. I slid a wet finger toward his sweet spot until I found that magic button of his. I swirled my finger around it while still sucking his cock every inch of it. He was writhing on the bed, on his back, placing his asshole strategically in the area of my probing finger.

"I need to make love to you," I said, gently moving my hand over his hard dick, still swirling around that hole I craved.

"I need you too," he whispered. "How would you like to take me? What would please you most?" he asked with eagerness.

"I have an idea I've been fantasizing about for a while now. Grab your lube and stand up, stud," I growled, sliding to the edge of the bed.

Kai hopped out of bed and opened the nightstand, grabbing the lube and a condom. I walked around the bed and sat down on the floor in front of him. "Come here handsome."

He stood in front of me without question. I nudged his legs apart and placed my hands on his hips, and pulled him closer so I could take his erection back into my mouth. I wanted to get him worked up again before I showed him how much I desired him. While he fucked my face, I rubbed his perfect ass with one hand while my other found his hot spot again. My lubed finger pressed until he allowed me to pass into his warmth.

"Yes… that feels good, Wyatt. Keep sucking my cock and finger fuck me too."

I knew he was in heaven when he let his head lean back and he thrust forward into my waiting mouth. I began to sink my finger deeper into him, moving it around to prepare it for my

THIRTY-TWO: WYATT

huge cock that I'd be providing any minute. My swollen dick was protruding and dripping from the excitement. Pushing back into Kai, I moved the heavily lubed finger around and pulled it back out. He bucked against my fingers under his crack, begging for me to get back at it. This time I slid two fingers in to stretch him some more, making sure he'd be able to accommodate my entire cock.

"Can you handle three?" I asked, looking up at him.

Kai angled his face down to catch my eyes, he was biting his lip. "Yes," he moaned, shivering with desire. He bobbed his head up and down, confirming his answer again.

I slid a third finger in very carefully, giving him time to absorb another digit before I began to move in and out of him. He bucked his hips from the thrill of being prodded by my fingers and his cock twitched in my mouth.

"You want some dick in there yet? Can you handle all of my thick cock?" I asked, sounding a bit threatening in my questioning. "Because I have a desire that I need you to fulfill, can you do that?" I snarled in a whisper.

He shook his head up and down. His eyes were wide, anticipating more pleasure. He was allowing me to use him for my carnal desire. He was mine right then and there and he wanted to be shown what I had planned next.

I moved to sit on the edge of the bed, my cock stood up long and thick. It didn't hang left or right as it was engorged fully, upright, and was brick hard. I slowly sheathed it in a condom and lubed up my hand, rubbing my full length up and down as Kai watched me with hungry eyes. I stroked myself for a few extra seconds so he could enjoy the teasing.

"Straddle me," I demanded, tapping my lap. "I want you to face me and wrap your legs around my waist.

He did as he was told. His ass rested on my lap while he had his legs wrapped around my waist with his entire weight resting on my knees. Our cocks finally touched as they met between us. I reached my hand around both of them, stroking them in unison. We kissed deeply and he moaned as I continued to manipulate both of our dicks. When I had him moaning and writhing on me, I lifted him and slipped my cock under his asshole. My lubed shaft slid near his hole, and he groaned in anticipation of what was to come.

Keeping him lifted, I positioned the head of my swollen tool at his hole. "Slide down and take me inside," I whispered, burning desire in my voice.

We faced each other and our eyes connected as he used his hand to guide my cock into his hole. I held his gaze as I felt him slide further down my pole, a determined look on his face because his body was still adjusting to my invasion. His eyes rolled back as he opened up fully. When he had all of me in him, we paused for a passionate kiss that threatened to take my breath away. I slowly ground my hips into him, stretching his hole and trying to get deeper.

"You're beautiful Kai. I've never felt this… this much desire for someone. It's always been just sex, but you and me, this is just so much more than that."

Kai wrapped his arms around my neck as he moved up and down, pleasure rolled across his face like a wave on the shore. He laid his head into the crook of my neck and moaned with desire, his breath a warm caress on my skin.

"Take all of me, Wyatt. I'm yours, I need you to make love to me like this, use my body as your own. I love you inside of me," he whispered into my neck.

I wrapped my arms around him tightly, needing him as close

as possible. He started biting my neck, sending more pleasure coursing through me. Our rhythm was getting faster as he bounced up and down on my lap.

Grabbing his dick, I began to stroke him because my balls were aching for release. Kai began to move faster, grinding himself on my lap, welcoming me to plunge harder and deeper into him. He pulled his face from my neck and stared directly into my eyes. He searched my face, needing something from me. I wasn't sure what it was that he sought since we were connecting in the most intimate of ways. I was in him; he was accepting my powerful urges as we both fulfilled our needs.

With a hooded gaze, Kai leaned closer and we melted into each other's mouths, our tongues exploring. I thrust my cock faster into him, and his hips came down harder with every stroke.

"Come on Wyatt, give it to me harder," he moaned, his mouth tight as he gritted his teeth.

I held him tight and knew I was close to release. "I love being with you," I said, staring at his delirious face.

"I love being with you too" He smiled at me, and his face showed an emotion I wasn't prepared for.

"You do?" I asked.

"Yeah, I do. Since the first day, I saw you. I knew I wanted this... wanted you."

I was overcome with emotion and held him tight. I stood up and he instinctively kept his legs wrapped around me, gripping my cock with his hole when I laid him across the bed.

"Make love to me Wyatt," he whispered into my ear.

Placing my hands on both sides of his face, I kissed him and I moved inside him with gentle strokes, my cock sinking in deeper when he opened himself completely to me.

"I love you, Kai," I whispered, and I meant it. I stared down at his sweet face. I was full of joy and hope for the first time in a long time.

"I love you too."

The admission of our feelings for each other only heightened our lovemaking. I plunged deeper into him, and we melted into one body in a frenzied passionate session of lovemaking.

"It feels… so good," he moaned when his cock rubbed against my stomach. "I'm close, give it to me harder."

I moved my hips faster against his, sensing my release was near. Our sweat-covered bodies moved in perfect harmony.

"I'm coming… holy fuck," I yelled, trying to stifle my groan, my body tensed when I shot my last bit of orgasm into him.

Kai was bucking under me, and he let loose a loud groan when his load shot between us, covering us both.

We laid still, connected as one while we caught our breath and melted into each other. I didn't care about the sweat, the lube, or the sticky mess from our orgasms. Nothing else mattered.

"I meant what I said Kai, I love you. I want you to be mine."

"I meant what I said too. I love you and want to be yours."

Thirty-Three: Wyatt

This Soldier Is Finally Home

Four Months Later

The streets of Kabul were quiet and all I could see was smoke curling around the war-torn street. An image appeared at a distance and a silhouette of a man emerged. I hurried toward him, placing my arms around him, "Jim!"

"Hey, Wyatt," he pulled away and looked at me.

"I'm sorry I couldn't save you."

"I know you are buddy, but I'm okay now. I am in a better place," he said, the solace in his voice was a contrast to the fear and pain I used to know. "Kai is a keeper," he continued.

"He is and I love him. I finally know how it feels to be happy," I admitted.

"I can see that, Wyatt. You deserve to be happy after everything you've been through."

"Thank you, Jim. I wish you could've met him."

"Me too. But Wyatt?" he paused and put his hand on my shoulder. "You're gonna have to let me go now." Jim backed up before I was able to say anything. He was right, I needed to let him go.

"Until we meet again brother," I whispered.

***

The light coming from the full moon beamed through the window of our bedroom, giving the place an ethereal glow and cast shadows on Kai's beautiful face while he slept. His features were softer when he was sleeping.

He shimmied a bit before he turned to lie onto his side, using his left arm as a pillow.

I held my breath, careful not to make any noise because I didn't want to wake him. This new angle of him allowed me to cherish all of him, a habit I'd never tire of doing. His long eyelashes were resting on his cheeks and those red lips of his seemed to have a smile plastered to them permanently. I was tempted to kiss him so I could feel them once again, but for now, I was satisfied to just watch him.

Slowly, Kai opened his eyes and those gorgeous light brown eyes met mine. They seemed to have lights of their own as they sparkled even in the dark. The sight made me feel breathless. "Some people might call that creepy," he said, referring to me watching him sleep. His smile widening.

Jesus! How can someone be this beautiful? "I'm sorry, I didn't mean to freak you out."

"What is it?" he asked.

"I had a dream about Jim. He was alive and in a better place."

Kai scooted closer and rested his head on my chest. "That's different from the ones you usually have," he said while placing his hand on my chest. His thumb caressing gentle circles, soothing me.

After my impromptu visit to Hawai'i months ago, I was open with Kai about my dreams and therapy sessions. It had been

THIRTY-THREE: WYATT

scary at first, but I needed him to know the horrors I was experiencing and how I was trying to heal. I was so thankful that he still wanted me after showing him all the cuts and scars I hid. "It was. I think he was letting me go too."

"How does that make you feel?"

"You sound like my therapist," I teased before continuing. "It makes me feel free if that makes any sense."

"It does, baby," Kai looked up and kissed my jaw.

"Let's go back to sleep, we have an early day tomorrow."

"I love you, Wyatt."

"I love you too, Kai."

"Uncle Wyatt, can I take this with me?" Elijah asked while he showed me his colorful kite that matched his life vest.

"Of course, bud. Uncle Kai can help you later," I told him and he ran to the boat dragging the small kite on the ground.

"I can't believe we've never done this," Elizabeth squeaked, unable to hide her excitement. She hooked her arm around Avery who just finished loading the food for the cruise. We were about to celebrate the grand reopening of our new office with our families. Kai's innovative designs were awe-inspiring with ocean and island-inspired touches.

Kai's parents, who insisted on me calling them *Ma* and *Pa* within two days of meeting me, were in town with Mikaela and Lei. "I don't know, but I'm glad we're doing it now," I said, standing behind Kai with my arms wrapped around his neck and nuzzling the back of his head. It was my favorite thing to do with him... well my second favorite.

"Is everything loaded?" Kai asked, kissing my forearm.

"Yup, we just need to wait for everyone to get here," Avery

answered. "Wyatt, by the way, Foster will be in town next week and he'd like to meet up before his schedule gets busier."

"Who's Foster?" Kai asked Avery.

"He's one of our good friends. He's a professional snow skier. Like pretty kick-ass," Avery answered.

"He skis for Canada though, that traitor!" I joked.

"Right?" Avery agreed. "Anyways, you want to just meet up at our place, since you and Kai are still in the middle of moving?" he continued.

Kai and I had decided to move our relationship to the next level and agreed to move in together a couple of weeks ago. It took a lot of bribing, including tech lessons from Kai, to get his landlord Sam to let Kai out of the six-month lease he'd signed when we got back from Hawai'i four months ago. "That'll be great, thanks," I said. "Wait, he doesn't want to go skiing, right? We suck at skiing."

"No, he doesn't. Besides it's been too warm for skiing," Avery answered.

"I don't know... that guy seems to always find a place to ski, regardless of the weather," I argued.

"I've always wanted to try skiing," Kai said.

"You'd hate it. You're not a big fan of being cold. Don't mention it to him though," I warned.

Avery chuckled and shook his head. "Okay, I'll tell him that we will all meet at our place."

"We picked a great day to do this. It's chilly, but at least the sun's out," I said, and looked around the water and the dock. I remembered the place where Kai saw me that fateful night that changed the rest of my life. That evening seemed like a lifetime ago when I looked back on it. I still have attacks occasionally, but with Kai around, I can take all the madness the world can throw at me. He was the beacon that guided me when I was lost at sea.

"You okay?" Kai turned around to face me, his cheeks were red from the frigid winter breeze.

"Never been better," I answered and wondered where everyone had gone. "Where is everybody?" I asked. I'd been so lost in my thoughts that I hadn't noticed they'd hopped onto the boat.

"Elizabeth wanted to keep an eye on Elijah, so they went in and joined Mrs. Turnley, Sam and the Three Musketeers," Kai explained, pressing his lips on mine. "I love you, Lance Corporal."

"I love you more, Kai." I zipped up his jacket to keep him warm because he was shivering a bit from the cold.

"Not possible," he argued.

"Where do you want these carrot cupcakes?" Andrea asked when they arrived.

"Carrot *muffins*," Pete corrected.

Kai shook his head before answering. "You can bring those *cupcakes* inside," he said and pointed to the catamaran.

"Aloha boys," Ma and Pa called, waving to get our attention as they'd just arrived at the office. We hurried and met them at the entrance to the dock. Since winter tourism was slow, we ran a limited sailing schedule which meant I had more time to spend with Kai.

"Mijo," Mrs. Martinez called, just when we reached Ma and Pa. She and Jim's father were also celebrating with us.

After I'd kissed Ma and Pa, I went to meet Mr. and Mrs. Martinez so I could help them with the baskets of fruit they'd insisted on bringing even though we'd told them that we had plenty of food for everyone.

"You look great, Son," Sophia said after hugging me then passing me to Carlos once she released me.

"It's true Wyatt, you do. Thanks for inviting us over," Carlos added.

"Of course, I wanted you here. Why don't you go ahead, and I'll meet you over there," I pointed to the boat.

I stood back as I watched everyone, including Kai, join Elizabeth, Avery, and Elijah on the boat. It wasn't the family I was born into, but I was so thankful for the one I chose.

Kai turned around and a warm smile crossed his face.

I knew then that this soldier was finally home.

-The End-

About the Author

About The Author Garry Michael Garry Michael is a Seattle based author who loves the outdoors, fashion, documentaries and tennis. His imagination will take you to the grounds of the US Open and to the sun kissed beaches of Hawaii. His stories will feature sports, medicine, politics and a whole lot of love.

Follow him on Instragram @author_garry_michael to learn more about his current projects.

Also by Garry Michael

Break Point
Tennis's golden boy Travis Montgomery is at the apex of his life and his young career after winning the US Open yet, his mind and heart is somewhere else. Somewhere deep inside the closet of his past and the secrets he hides even from those who are the closest to him. He is flashing back on another time, another dream, and another love when he is reminded of the only success that eludes him.

Fresh out of medical school, Dr. Ashton Kennedy moves back to Seattle to complete his medical training and start the new beginning he has wanted since Travis walked away six years ago. The task is proving to be harder than he anticipated, especially when Travis returns waving a white flag.

What will happen when these two men meet again after six long years? Will Ashton get his questions answered or will Travis' ambition force him even deeper into the closet?

Heartfelt and sometimes comical, Break Point is a story about friendship, love, forgiveness and living an authentic life.

Made in the USA
Middletown, DE
01 September 2021